THE ADVENTURES OF APPLE JOHN
THE MAN – THE MYTH

Chick Ludwig

Chick Ludwig (1946–   )
ISBN: 979-8-3481-5396-0

First printing 2024

This book is dedicated to my friend John Taylor, who is the inspiration for these stories.

CONTENTS

FORWARD

I first met John Taylor when we moved to the mountains of North Carolina a few years ago. We had stopped at one of the many "apple stands" that border the roads around Hendersonville. I fell into a conversation with John as he rang-up our purchase. Little did I know that we would soon be attending the same church. We quickly became good friends, and I would spend many happy hours listening to his stories. It is from these stories that the character of Apple John would appear in his many adventures.

INTRODUCTION TO APPLE JOHN
(The Man, The Myth)

The first thing I want ya'll to know is that each of these Apple John stories is absolutely true. Well, maybe some facts have been fudged a bit, and names changed to protect the guilty. A few facts have been slightly modified, left out, or added for clarity. Other than that, it's all true!

Apple John is a real person. He lives near Hendersonville, North Carolina. I'd better describe him for you so you can picture him as I tell you of his adventures.

No one knows for sure why he is called "Apple John", but I suspect that it's because he is usually seen munching on an apple, with another handy in his back pocket. Nor does anyone know his age, and he's not telling. John is of medium height, has a gangling but strong body, with long legs and arms. He has penetrating light blue eyes that sparkle as he talks. His hair is grey, streaked with black, and long, slightly wispy, and hanging to just over his large ears, which jut out at a jaunty angle, without lobes, giving him a somewhat comical look. His nose is also rather large and bulbous. His chin is receding and slightly pointed below the thin, sensuous lips. His neck is long and red from constant exposure to the mountain sunlight. Over his eyes that always seem locked in a penetrating stare, are thick, black, wooly-worm eyebrows. To offset his brows and hide his chin, he wears a ragged, unkempt beard. It is long, reaching to the top of the dingy farmer's coveralls that he always wears over a ragged, red flannel shirt, with faded pink long-johns underneath. On his feet are worn-out aviator boots left from his days as an aircraft mechanic aboard the USS Crash-a-lot, the Piper Cub aircraft carrier that was posted in the Gulf of Tongkin just off the Viet Nam coast. The end of the right boot has a hole, through which pokes his big toe. He never wears socks. He says that real men don't need socks. Bare feet make him strong. He sometimes uses his big toe, with its horny toenail to scratch the perpetual rash he has on his other ankle.

You would need to search a long way back in the mountains to find his house, but I can tell you that it is way out beyond Worlds Edge, near the top of Hickory Nut Falls. You can't see Rumbling Bald from his place, but you can hear it. He made me promise not to tell y'all more than that.

His house, if you can call it that, is a one room log cabin that a long-distant great-grandpappy built. John has kept it in good repair, and it is almost free of roof leaks. Even the gaps between the logs of the walls where the ancient chinking has fallen out have been carefully covered with cardboard. There is an old iron stove against one wall that not only heats the cabin, but serves as his cooking stove. The smoke stack is at an angle and pokes through what used to be a window. Along another wall is his pantry, stacked high with cans of every sort of edibles that he buys on sale at Aldi's. His favorite meal is deep fried Vienna Sausage, which he claims was invented by a distant cousin of his that was a pirate that had been shipwrecked over on the Pamlico sound during a hurricane.

You would expect that a hillbilly would consume Carolina Gold moonshine, but John drinks strictly Real Southern Sweet Tea. As a matter of fact, he makes annual trips to Florida to swap apples for a load of sugarcane to make sugar for his tea.

I see that I've wandered away a bit in describing John's living arrangements. So, let's get back to them right now. Directly across from the pantry is his bed. It's homemade and has ropes woven through holes in the sides that stretch somewhat tautly across it in two directions, supporting a mattress stuffed from the leaves stripped from sugarcane stalks. His blanket is an old one that his Indian ancestors made from turkey hide, and that has been handed down for multiple generations. He doesn't use sheets. Sheets are sissified, he states. In the center of the room is a three-legged table with the fourth corner propped up on field stones. A single candle, stuck on an overturned tin can, is his only source of light. Under the table he stores a five-gallon pickle bucket of water for washing his hands. It is changed every two weeks. He uses his Southern Swiss Army multi-tool pocket knife to eat with. In place of a chair is a single apple crate that he drug home when the dilapidated rocker he used to sit in collapsed one night as he was eating his supper.

The "necessary room" is a rickety outhouse behind the cabin that has a traditional crescent moon carved in the door for ventilation. The carved moon is strategically placed so John can peek out while doing his business to be sure no-one is sneaking around the cabin.

A mountain dulcimer leans in one corner of the cabin, and John sometimes picks a tune out on it before bed time, even though it only has two strings.

Apple John has never been married, but prefers the company of his faithful coon-hound that accompanies him everywhere he goes. John never names his dogs, but prefers to just call them "Dog". He only has one at a time, and he replaces it when it finally dies with a new puppy from a litter that has been bred true from the earliest members of the breed that began as companions of Indians.

John also enjoys watching the squirrels and other critters that feast on the scraps that John tosses out for them after every meal. He purposely makes too much food, just so he'll have leftovers for them. Sometimes he'll sit out on an old stump, strumming his dulcimer and singing to the top of his high, raspy voice, with his friendly old dog howling accompaniment. They are joined by the hundreds of little birds who live in the giant old red oak tree that overshadows the cabin. John attracts them by feeding them from the pocketfulls of apple seeds that he saves from the countless apples that he consumes each day.

John is a churchgoing man, and serves as deacon at the *Second Big Hungry Foot Stompin', Snake Handling Church.* He told me once that his mamma named him after the Apostle John from the Bible. He carries a copy of the Authorized Southern King James Version of the

Bible in his back pocket. Not the same pocket with the apple, but the one on the other side. He likes to quote verses about fruit from the Bible, saying how that it is always apples. If he knows you well enough, he'll relate that the wine Jesus served at the last supper was made from apples, not grapes as is commonly taught.

No one around here knew John until just after the end of the Viet Nam War. At that time, he began showing up around town in Hendersonville and surrounding communities. He soon became popular with the folks that enjoyed listening to his stories. He rarely talks about his personal life, but by paying careful attention to his stories, it is possible to deduce a little of his family tree.

Apparently, his ancestors migrated here from the coast along with the first white settlers. We know from his Indian blanket that there were Indians in his family line. Other hints point toward a relationship with men that were once a part of Blackbeard's crew that escaped the notorious pirate's capture at Ocracoke so many years ago. We'll probably never know all there is to know about Apple John, but it's enjoyable trying to ferret out clues from his many stories.

It is a matter of speculation what he does to earn money to live on, but it is rumored that he inherited some gold from one of his piratical forbears. He used to tell of a pirate chest full of gold hidden somewhere near his cabin, buried beneath an old cedar tree. No one has heard him relate that particular tale in many years. Speculation about it is that either it was a made-up story, or that it was true, but John became afraid that folks would try to find the chest. At any rate, he does tend a small orchard of stunted crab-apple trees that crowd around his cabin. Perhaps enough apples are left over to sell for a few dollars to provide him his meager living.

To wrap up this brief background about Apple John, I'll just say that John loves telling stories about his adventures. He remembers everything that has ever happened in his life. People's names, places, dates, down to the smallest detail. He can even remember his moment of birth! He also can tell you about other people's adventures. He is a vast storehouse of facts about every conceivable subject. Often, when I've come up against an insurmountable obstacle in my search for facts to support my *Chick Tales*, John will come to the rescue. His policy is to ALWAYS have an answer, even though he doesn't know what the answer is. As he always tells me, "Chick, if I cain't honestly give you an answer, I'll make one up." And he has never failed to do so.

2. APPLE JOHN'S FLYING DOG
(A Doggone Good Apple John Story)

Many of you folks here in the mountains know Apple John, but not many of you know about his old coon hound that he used to have during the Turkey Creek revival years. John isn't really much of a hunter, because he loves all of God's creatures, great and small. But he also loves hunting dogs. He had this great big coon hound that he trained to run really fast. He was SO fast that no coon could ever get away from him. Once on the trail, that old hound would quickly run Mr. Coon down and chase him up a tree. John would eventually catch up, wave to the coon saying, "Today's your lucky day, old feller.", and then he and the smiling dog would just turn around and head for home.

Now, this one time, his coon dog sighted the biggest old he-coon he'd ever seen, gave a sharp bark to let his master know, and the chase was on! The old coon, who had done this a time or two, was mighty fast, too. As a matter of fact, he was so fast that the old hound had to chase him clear down to Tumble Bug Creek near the Sacanon community! You all know that's WAY beyond yonder! Well, John had trained the old dog well, and that he was never to give up. And John would never give up either. The big dog finally caught up with that speedy coon, and chased him up a big ol' red oak tree where he remained hiding and trembling with fear. John's faithful hound remained at the base of the tree, howling at the coon until John finally drug up wheezing and gasping from fatigue. As was John's custom, he admiringly waved at the perplexed coon, and he and the happy dog turned for home.

As you can guess, John was mightily worn out as they trudged out the old Sugarloaf Road back towards home at Worlds Edge. Pretty soon, along came an old Ford pick-up piled high with a load of hay, and John decided then and there that he'd just flag it down and ask for a

11

ride. The driver replied "Sure, I'll give ya a ride, but there ain't no room for your dog." To which John replied, "That's ok, my old dog is plenty fast and will just run alongside." So, John climbed aboard and off they went. They got up to 35 miles an hour, and the driver asked how the dog was doing. John said, "Thar he is." And pointed out the window, and there was the hound loping along, not even breathing hard, so the driver sped up to 55 mph. Presently, he asked again how the dog was doing. Again, John replied that he was doing fine.

It was just about then that they reached the turn before the cliff that gives World's Edge its name. The panicked driver slammed on the brakes. As the old truck slid to a stop, the dog went flying past the driver's window and sailed over the edge! But then, just as the startled driver was about to apologize to John for sending the old dog to his death, a mighty unexpected thing happened. A parachute popped open! "What's this?" The man exclaimed. "I could see that your dog was fast, but I never expected to see him fly!

To this, John replied, "Yep, always happens right here. I've been atrainin' him to be fast, but I jest ain't agotten 'round to teach him how to STOP fast!"

3. APPLE JOHN AND THE SILO
(Another Really Fast Apple John Story)

It's time to tell y'all another story about Apple John. Maybe you won't believe me, but it's all true. I guarantee it. Several years ago, there was a farmer down around Sacanon who was needing to clear some old structures from his holdings to make way for a new field of tomatoes he was adding to take the place of some of his old apple trees that had died of an early winter freeze. Right smack in the middle of the area he wanted cleared was a great big old silo. He wanted it out of there, so he began looking around for someone to knock it down. He asked in Edneyville, but no one wanted the job. He went on down to the old country store in Dana, but no one knew of anyone there either, but someone suggested that he had heard of a man from out in World's Edge that just might tackle a dangerous job like that.

The farmer wandered on up to Worlds Edge and commenced to asking around. He finally found an old feller who allowed as he just might know someone who might take it on, and said the man was known as Apple John. The farmer soon found John napping out under an old cedar tree with his faithful dog. You know, the same one I told y'all about in another story, that chased down that old coon. Anyway, John said it was a mighty dangerous thing to knock down an old silo, but he thought as how he was up to the job. The only way to do it was to go inside with a big sledge hammer and knock out most of the bricks in the bottom few layers, leaving just enough to hold everything in place. Then you could give one more swing of the sledge on one side and everything would just collapse upon itself. You'd have to be awfully fast to get out from under before it fell. Now as y'all know, Apple John is a humble man, but he is also justifiably proud of how fast he can run. He had to be quick to stay within ear shot of his old coon hound. As a matter of fact, John is known far and wide as the fastest runner in all Henderson County.

So, let's get on with the story and see how this all works itself out. When we left off, the farmer was talking with John about the upcoming piece of work. After some good country negotiating, an agreement was reached. It was decided that John would be at the farmer's place first thing next morning. As always seems to happen in the country, word soon got around, and folks began showing up before dawn to see what's what. Sure enough, just as daylight was making itself known, Good old John came sauntering up, whistling a happy tune. After a cheerful, "Mornin,' y'all," he ducked into the rustic old silo and commenced knocking bricks out. Meanwhile, folks began discussing among themselves if John really WAS the fastest man in the county, and would he be able to get out safely. I'm a bit ashamed to say it, but bets were even laid on the outcome!

Eventually John's voice rang out, "THAR SHE GOES!" and he took to running. But there was his old dog carelessly lying on the floor, and as luck would have it, he got himself all tangled up as the Silo tumbled down around him! All anyone could see was a great cloud of dust and debris billowing up from the scene. There was no sign of poor John. Everyone feared the worst, and as it was getting dark, they just turned for home, figuring that they'd come back the next day to search for old John and take his mortal remains home for a Christian burial.

Dawn came peacefully the next day. The early morning red was just giving way to a beautiful Carolina-blue sky. Folks gathered and soon noticed that the old farmer was humming a happy tune to himself as he loaded the crumbled remains of the silo into his old farm wagon. One gentleman, less timid than the rest, went up to the farmer asking, "What happened? Why are you so happy? Did John make it out? Is he REALLY the fastest runner in the county?" To which the old farmer replied, "Well son. I don't know if John is the fastest runner or not, but he sure as heck can CRAWL mighty fast!

4. APPLE JOHN AND SOME SPRING TIME FUN
(Another Fun Apple John Story)

It was a beautiful, warm early spring morning. I'd just reached my old friend Apple John's cabin and noticed that he was pretty cranky and mumbling to himself. "John, what's the matter?", I asked.

"Dang flatlanders", he exclaimed before resuming his mumbling.

I knew his disdain for anyone that wasn't born and raised in the mountains. It had taken several months and trips up the old crumbling wagon road to his cabin out in the Big Hungry area near World's Edge for him to trust me enough to even talk to me. But by now we had become good friends. "So, tell me what happened to get you so upset."

He growled and scratched himself on the seat of the ragged farmer's cover-alls he always wore, banged his corn cob pipe against the other leg, and pulled a fist full of bakker from the pocket of the tattered flannel shirt he wore winter and summer. After much grumbling and fussing while stuffing the bakker into the black, crusted bowl of his pipe, he pulled a match from the other pocket of his shirt, struck it on his pants in the spot he had just been scratching and lit the pipe. He took a long puff, blew it out, and began his tale. "Well, I'll tell ya, young-un. Ya knows that crooked spot on the road on the way up to my place?"

"Do you mean the spot that folks used to slide over the edge at before you put the fence up?

"Yep, that thar's the one." He barked. "Some 'blankity-blank' (Sometimes John uses language that is not suitable for young ears—or eyes.) was a-comin' up to swim in my old swimmin' hole down on the Big Hungry."

"So, what's wrong with that? I know you don't mind people doing that."

"Yeah, but that dang fool flatlander done gone and went over the edge."

"But John, what about the fence? Didn't he see that?"

Old John got that squinty-eyed look he gets when he suspects that

15

I've caught him in something. He puffed out a big cloud of black smoke and continued, "Jest hold on to yore suspenders. I was just a-gittin to that very thang." With that, John shuffled his feet a bit, and looking sheepisly at the floor, he went on, "I heard a great commotion and hollerin acomin' from over that way, so's I scurried over to see what was a-goin' on. Just as I got thar, the durn fool was a-climin' up over the edge. He hollered at me and asked me why thar warn't no fence up thar."

"But John, there was a fence."

To this, my friend replied, "No thar ain't. In all the years that dang fence was thar, ain't nobody never done gone over, so's I figured it warn't needed so I tore it down!"

By now, old John had settled himself down and we spent some time talking about the roads here in the mountains.

I like to say how the curves on some of the roads are so tight that if you weren't careful, you'd run into the back of your own car. As always, we'd have a good laugh at the same old worn-out jokes. After my friend chuckled at that, and snorting a little, he said, "Does ya know what the sides of the mountain are called on either side of the road?"

"No John, what are the sides of the road called." Of course, I knew the answer since we had asked each other that same question many times before. Poor John was about to bust. He could hardly contain himself as he burst out with, "The mountain side goes up, and the sui-side goes down!" With that, he slapped his thigh and burst out with a loud guffah and almost fell out of his old rocking chair. Then we just sat quietly thinking to ourselves for a few minutes. I could see that John was working himself up to pick up the conversation again. Pretty soon I could tell that he was about ready to come out with one of his tales of his early years. His face always gets a little pink, and he gets little wrinkles around his eyes. Well, in addition to the ones he always has. Then his faded blue eyes get a special sparkle as he starts talking.

"I been thinkin' about that ol' swimmin' hole we was talkin' about before. We-uns kids shore did have a great time down thar! We's couldn't wait 'til summer to go skinny dippin' after our chores was done."

"Skinny dipping, John? Weren't you embarrassed?" As soon as I said that, I knew I was in trouble.

My friend burst out laughing, spewing out a lung full of smoke. "Well young-un---of course we was all bare-assed! That's the way ya goes skinny dippin'! Anyhows, warn't nobody thar ceptin' us boys."

Then he chortled to himself a bit more before continuing.

"We-uns couldn't wait 'til the first warm day of spring. Then we'd all meet up on that little beach area, strip off our clothes, and hang them on a saplin' before diving in the cold water. We'd spend all day thar swimmin' ans asplashin' each other, and throwing gobs of mud at each other. Long 'bout the time the Sun was agettin' low, we'd head off yonder to home."

"Gosh, John, sounds like you guys had a great time."

"Yep, we shorely did!" Then he got a thoughtful look, furrowed up his brow, and said, "Onliest one problem. We done stayed thar so long that we got us a bad sunburn. Had to stay in the cabin for a coupla weeks til it all peeled off."

"Wow, John, that musta hurt!"

"Yep, but we-alls made the best of it. We'd all try to peel the biggest patch of skin off and compare it at school next day. Then we'd put all our patches together. and the boy with the biggest patch got to choose the girl and stash it all in her desk when she waren't lookin'. Shore was fun when she'd find it and let out a screech! We-uns would laugh and carry on so much that we'd all hafta stand in the corner, and stay after school and clean the blackboard an stuff."

"You were just being boys I guess. But didn't you hate having to stay after school?"

"Nope, couldn't go out in the sun noways with them sunburns. Besides that, we got out of our afternoon chores at home."

"You sure knew how to have fun back in those days, didn't you?"

"Yep, we shore did. And the fun ain't over yet! How's 'bout we head down to the crick for some skinny dippin' right now, young-un?"

"I don't think so, John!" I said as I shuddered at the thought of old John "nekked".

5. APPLE JOHN AND THE RACE BOAT
(Another Racy Apple John Story)

The other day I was over near World's Edge visiting my friend Apple John. I was telling him about my new boat that I have been building and He asked me how I got interested in boats in the first place, so I told him about how as a young-un, I used to race boats. You know, those little hydroplanes with a big Mercury motor on them. Now this story is not actually about John, but he had heard it from the old men that would gather around the old potbellied stove at the hardware store. Before he got started, he pulled a big, juicy red delicious apple out of his coveralls and polished it with the stained handkerchief he always carries around in his hip pocket. After methodically wiping it all over, he wiped his nose on the old rag and absentmindedly stuffed it back in his pocket.

He then launched into a story about a time not long after Lake Lure was first filled up. "Young-un, (John always calls me young-un, even though I'm almost his age.) let me tell y'all about this feller that lived down in the town of Lake Lure. Musta been in the early 1930s or so. As I recall, his name was Riley, Rally, somethin' likens that. I don't rightly recollect no more. Anyways, let's just call him Rally."

John proceeded with his story and was just getting warmed up good in the telling. Seems that Rally had heard about folks dropping car engines into boats and racing each other, just for kicks. Now Rally was kinda a wild young-un and thought that sounded like something he'd like to do. He cogitated over it for a while and decided he could not possibly live another year if he couldn't have one of his very own. He took an old jon boat and stuffed a big Ford flat head-eight in her. No exhaust muffler, so it was powerful loud. Showed it off prouder than a bull frog singin' on a lily pad. His bestest friend was named Boomer Loudin, and he liked fast hot rods. Always blastin' around the mountain roads in one. They got to bragging to each other about whether the car, or the boat was the fastest. Finally, Boomer bet him five bucks he could beat him in a race around the back side of the lake to where the road ended at Old Uncle John's place. Old Uncle John was Apple John's namesake.

Only thing to do was to haul his new boat down to the lake. Dropped it off the back of his pick-um up truck. Climbed aboard, and lit 'er up. VROOOM-POP-POW-VROOM... People ran, babies cried, dogs bellowed, horses scattered. They took off down the lake together, Boomer in his jalopy on the dirt road that ran around the shore, and Rally in the jon boat along-side the shore, dodging around rocks the whole time so he could stay close to lake. Rally was hanging on for dear life itself! He'd just about get settled down on the seat when he'd have to dodge a rock, and he'd bounce way up in the air, hanging on to the steering wheel with nothing but his fingernails! Turns out that the boat was faster, even with having to dodge boulders in the water. The car was getting bogged down in the ruts of the old wagon road.

Eventually Rally was coming close to Uncle John's place. Now, they hadn't figured on old John's reaction. Apple John explained how Uncle John had lived his whole life over on the mountain above Lake Lure before there even was a Lake. He was an old recluse. Never went to town---too loud. Liked peace and quiet. He loved the birds singing, the bees buzzing, the crickets chirping. He had lived with his wife, Bessie, in the old log cabin that they had built with their own hands, way up the side of the mountain before lake was filled. Now he had himself water-front property! The lake was so new that neither one of them had ever seen a motor boat before.

John had just finished his lunch of pork-belly followed up with several swigs of his special "shine" before moseying down to sit on a big boulder under an old oak tree overhanging the lake—to take a little snooze. He was just about to drift off when he heard a powerful loud noise coming from down the lake. VROOM-VROOOM! He peered down the shoreline but couldn't see anything. Being a little near sighted, he hollered for Miss Bessie to come take a look. When she came running up, he said, "Whaddaya suppose it is? It sounds horrible!" "Maybe it's Rumblin'Bald a-shiftin'!" (I'd better explain right here that Rumblin Bald is the name of the mountain that they lived on. Occasionally over the years, it would shake and rumble from an earth quake. Folks in the old days thought there was a great monster living deep underground in a cave, that was making the noise.)

"Do ya think it could be a lake monster?", Bessie asks. "Heck-fire no.," replies John. "Lake ain't been here nowhere long enough to have a monster in it."

Meanwhile, the racket is getting closer and closer! Now they can see water splashing and spraying everywhere! Then, as it comes around the bend, they can see some poor guy flopping up above the spray.

"Woman, go git me my shot gun from offen the wall! Run now, hurry it up!"

As soon as she comes huffing and puffing back with his trusty gun, he fires off both barrels. Pieces of the boat went every which-a-way! The motor went that-away, and Rally went yet other! Bessie hollered, "Whaddaya think it was? Did ya kill it?" To which old John replied, "I don't rightly know, but whatever it was, at least I made it let go of that poor feller."

6. APPLE JOHN AND THE NAVY DOCTOR
(Another Ship-Shape Apple John Story)

I was visiting my friend Apple John the other day at his cabin out at World's Edge. It's a long hike from where I have to park my car, but a pretty one with the spring blossoms coming out on his crab apple trees next to the babbling "crick". I found old John on his front porch in his rocker, leaning back against the cabin wall. His old dog, named "Dog", was snuggled up close. I noticed that John had his coveralls and long johns rolled up and a dirty rag wrapped around his leg. When I asked what happened, he guffawed and told me that he was carrying some wood in for his stove and had tripped over Dog. We had a good laugh over that. Then he said that it reminded him of a couple of funny incidents back in his Navy days as an aircraft mechanic aboard the *USS Crashalot*, the Piper Cub aircraft carrier, during the Viet Nam conflict.

Seems that one day during a break in the usual wartime activities, the skipper suggested that John pull the engine out of the Cub and clean it up. Well, he did just that. He mounted the engine on a test stand to work on it. Then he rolled it into the mess hall where it was clean and he'd have plenty of room. When he was finished, he thought it would be a good idea to fire up the engine to be sure he hadn't gotten water into some vital area. Fortunately, the propeller was still mounted. Actually, flipping the prop was the only way to start the engine that powered the old plane.

John grabbed hold of the blade and gave a mighty flip. Off she roared! Only one small problem with that. It was then that he realized his mistake! The stand was not fastened down! Off the whole contraption went across the deck! Not wanting to lose the valuable engine overboard, he grabbed the engine stand and held on with all he was worth! But all to no avail. The engine pulled the stand, John, and all, breaking the sliding glass door as it continued onto the flight deck, and flopped over, thereby stopping the engine. Unfortunately,

John was cut pretty badly and the barber/doctor (Everyone did double duty on the boat---I mean ship.) Had to come get John and take him to get him bandaged up. While he was gone, the cook cleaned up the spilled gasoline with paper towels to use as rags and threw them into the toilet. I mean head. (On a ship, the toilet is called a "head".)

When John got back from the doctor's ministrations, he went into the head and sat down to do his business. He thought it would be a good time to light up his pipe, so he pulled out a match to light up, and absentmindedly tossed the still glowing match into the toilet. KA-BOOM! The gas-soaked rags exploded! Back came the doc and his helper. They loaded him up on the door of the privy (What Southern boys called the head.) that had been blown off its hinges, and headed off. Then they got to laughing so hard that they dropped poor John and broke his leg!

We had a good laugh over that story, when old John said he had another amusing incident to relate. With John, one story always seems to lead to another, and I've learned to wait for him to finish. I waited while John pulled some "baccer" (That's what John calls his tobacco.) out of the pocket of his old, tattered flannel shirt that he wears winter and summer. After tamping it in the bowl of his trusty old corncob pipe, he lit up and proceeded to relate this latest tale.

It was another slow time in the fighting action, and the *Crashalot* was back at its dock, but the crew had to stay aboard. The skipper was afraid to let them go ashore since they always seemed to get into some ruckus or another when they did. It had only been a day or two but the guys were getting bored with whittling popsickle sticks and trying to outdo each other with tall tales. They would have spent the time fishing, but the captain wouldn't even allow them ashore to dig up night crawlers for bait. After much deliberation, they came upon a scheme. One of the fellas had been down to Cypress Gardens in sunny Florida, and watched the water ski show. They could do that! But they had no ski-boat. What to do? Well, John had an answer. Why not use the Piper Cub that he was mechanic for to pull the skier? Great idea!

(I'd better tell y'all that floats had been attached to the Cub before it was brought aboard as a scout plane.) So, they did just that. They snuck a spare dock line from the locker it was stored in to use as a tow rope, salvaged a couple of boards that were aboard to patch up the boat—I mean ship—when it got damaged from enemy action, or running into the lake shore by accident. They tied the boards to the feet of the brave sailor who had volunteered to go first, and off they went.

They were having a great time! Pretty soon the skier noticed some pretty WAVES standing on the dock watching. (I'd better stop right here again and explain that in the navy, girls were called "WAVES". Maybe because the guys always waved at them. Just like in the army they're called "WACS" because all the boys act wacky around them.) But now let's get back to our fascinating story. They decided the only thing they could possibly do to impress the girls was to ski close enough to spray them down! The plane roared past the dock pulling the excited skier behind. The poor boy was SO excited that he ran right into the pilings holding the dock up! The worst part of the whole deal was that the force of the collision knocked his arm slap off!

The guys all rushed over, pulled him out of the water, and laid him out on the dock. Then they called the base hospital that had been established in an old abandoned hamburger stand. While waiting for the old Anglia car that served as an ambulance, they found the arm, still clutching the handle of the tow rope, and looked around for something to put it in. One of them saw a cooler on the edge of the dock. He retrieved it and brought it over. Perfect! It even had a six-pack of "Pepsi" on ice in it. (No conscientious Christian Southern sailor boy would ever admit to being in possession of anything containing spirits!) They unloaded the "Pepsi" and respectfully put the arm in the cooler, and set it out of the way while they consumed the "Pepsi".

Eventually the ambulance rumbled up and they loaded the poor sailor in. But when they went for the cooler, it had vanished! Arm and all! They immediately called the base sheriff. (Being a base populated by nothing but good old country boys, they had a sheriff rather than MPs.) Luckily, he caught a couple of civilians trying to carry the cooler home, thinking they had stolen only "Pepsi". He arrested them on the spot and charged them.

It was right here that old John stopped his narrative, looked right at me, and with a mischievous twinkle in his eye, asked, "Young-un, (John always calls me "young-un".) what do you think the sheriff charged 'em with?" I allowed that I had no earthly idea. After a mite of time to build suspense, he said, "Well, I'll tell ya. It was ARMED ROBBERY!"

John swears on his old Authorized Southern King James bible that both stories are one hundred percent true! You be the Judge.

Note: I see a couple of you looked confused when you read the word "Pepsi." I'm sure if you are a Southern boy, you always drink Pepsi Cola rather than the inferior Coca Cola. But why the " " around Pepsi. You didn't really think that any kind of "cola" was in that cooler, did you?

7. APPLE JOHN REWRITES HISTORY
(Another Historically Accurate Apple John story)

I was talking to my friend Apple John a few days ago when we happened to be occupying the same bench on Main Street. I was telling him about a book that I'm reading called, *From the Banks of the Oklawaha*, by Frank FitzSimons, and how much I enjoyed learning about the history of Hendersonville and the surrounding area. John gave a little laugh like he does when he's amused by something someone says. Actually, it is more of a snicker, ending in a snort.

He replied, "Young-un," John always calls me young-un even though I'm almost as old as he is. "I knew Frank well, and listened to his program on WHKP most days, but, I gotta tell ya, he didn't have all of his facts right. I oughta know. My family was here during the time when all of these things took place. Let me straighten it out for ya." He then proceeded to set in to do just that. All I could do was take a deep breath and settle back on the bench.

"First off, William Mills claimed to have been the first white settler here in the mountains. The truth is that he fled to the mountains in 1780, after fighting for the hated British. As a matter of fact, William Mills is said to have avoided capture after the Battle of Kings Mountain by playing dead while the Patriots were collecting prisoners, and he escaped to Sugar Loaf Mountain, where he hid in a cave for a period of time. I'm here to tell ya, he was NOT here first. My great, great, great—I don't know how many greats—grandpappy was here first! And he didn't have to run away to escape anything. He was already here. That cave is just up the stream apiece from my place. I've been in that old cave. And I have proof that grandpappy really was here first. If ya look just above the entrance inside the cave, carved in the ceiling, you'll see 'W. M. 1781'. Then if ya look a little higher, you'll find 'G.P.J.' carved in the rock. That stands for 'Grand Pappy John', and the date, '1775'. What better proof could you want?" That was only the first of

John's revelations. I could see he was lost in thought, so I just took a breath and made myself more comfortable, and waited to see what would happen next. Sometimes it takes old John awhile to bring the facts to the forefront of his mind. After a few minutes, he shifted himself a bit, cleared his throat, and began in his high pitched, raspy voice.

"And another thing. Mr. Frank tries to make us believe that the first 'lektrical generation plant was down on the Big Hungry River. He says that the ruins of the old dam are what you see from Big Hungry Road as you go over the bridge. Well, it just ain't so. In the first place, that road warn't even thar back then. I know -- I've been thar. That partic'lar dam is really the remains of the mill dam my family built back around the same time that power was first brung to Hendersonville. My great-great-great grand pappy John built it to make the mash for his special recipe of corn likker that everyone was so eager to get a sip of in them days."

I tried to get in a word or two here in defense of Mr. FitzSimons. I should have known that once John started in, there was no way to interrupt him, so I just did the only thing I could do. I shut up and listened. He cleared his throat, took a puff on his old corn cob pipe that he's always got in his hand, and took up where he had left off.

"I'm gonna tell ya the true story of how our little town got its first power plant. My great-great-great uncle Jack was the one who brought us our 'lectrickity. Here's the truth of the matter. You know that the Oklawaha crick runs all around town. Uncle Jack had his rug weaving factory right on the bank of the crick. He had dammed up the crick to make a pond to turn a paddle wheel to power his machinery, like was the way back then. Now old Jack was known as a bit of a tyrant in those days. He wanted to keep his crew working day and night. Trouble was that it cost him a big piece of his profits to buy enough candles to light the big shed so his folks could see what they was a-doin'. Kinda hard to weave rugs when ya cain't hardly see."

About this time, John noticed that his pipe had gone out. That happens to him a lot, but he never gets used to it. "THIS DANG GOL-DARN PIECE OF CORN-CERNED BLANKETTY-BLANK..."! he exclaimed in a voice loud enough that it woke up his old hound dog, "Dog", who had been sleeping soundly at his side. Dog just opened one eye, looked up as if to say, "Can't a dog get no dang sleep around here, no way?", Then he snorted and went back to sleep. I guess I'd better say right here that sometimes john will say words that aren't exactly supposed to be in a good Christian's vocabulary.

Finally, he wound down, sputtered a little, and reached into the pocket of his old flannel shirt and pulled out a fist full of his own special baccer as he calls it. He grows his own blend back on his little plot of land up near World's Edge over above Chimney Rock. First, he knocked out his pipe against the leg of his farmer's coveralls, then wiped the bowl clean with his left pointer finger. He told me once that he always uses his left pointer so he can keep the right one clean because that's the hand he plucks apple seeds out of his teeth with.

I see we've wandered away from the narrative a mite. John stuffed a liberal wad of the tobacco into the pipe and struck a match on the seat of his cover-alls and lit it. After a few puffs to get the baccer going good, he proceeded.

"It warn't long after lectrikity became popular in the late 1890s that rich folks in town wanted some for themselves. They had 'em a little generator up offa seventh, but it wouldn't hardly run nothin' a-tall. Had to burn oil to run it. Might as well just put the oil in lanterns. Jack got to figurin'. 'I got me this mill wheel out here in the crick turnin' my chinery. Why cain't ah use it to make lektrikity too?'"

John stopped here for a bit while he stirred his pipe a little and re-lit it. A common occurrence. Then he picked up where he had left off. "One dark and stormy night, Jack snuck hisself on up to the generator up town. He done took the whole dang thang and carted it back down to his mill. He ripped off the motor and tossed it aside, then stuck a big pulley on the shaft of the generatin' gizmo, and ran one of them big leather belts from his water wheel to it. That's when he discovered that he didn't have no lektrikle wire. No problem for a clever cuss like my uncle jack! He just used some old barbed wire he pulled from the fences the dang Yankees had strung up around their fancy houses to keep hard workin' folks' cows and pigs outa their yards."

Right here I tried to interrupt John to clear up a few details. It seemed to me that his story was stretching the bounds of believability a little, but he'd have none of it. Off he went again.

"When the folks in town saw what he had done, they all wanted them some of the lektrikity for themselves. Old Jack knew him a good thing when it stared him in the face, so he hooked them up too. Then he got them to pay him every month. Mostly bartered for eggs, milk, and stuff. Allwas workin' out real good until the dang city leaders decided to tax poor Jack. Now my old Uncle Jack, as I told ya, was kinda a cantankerous old feller, and warn't about to pay no taxes! He went out that very day and burned down his factry, busted up his dam, and moved back out to his family property at World's Edge where we'ums lived from then to this here very day. And THAT'S the truth of how the first real lektrikity came to town."

I thought that john had finished rewriting Hendersonville history, but he still had more to say. "And here's another thing Fitz got wrong. He tried to tell us that the land that Carl Sandburg lived on, Conamur---Connymera---dang, you know what I mean, was first owned by this guy, Christopher Gustav Memminger. He was a rich lawyer from down in Charleston that came up here to steal the mountains from us real mountain folks. Young-un, I'm agona tell ya the real story."

"You mean Connemara, Carl Sandburg's estate." I settled back on the bench and took another deep breath, and prepared myself for the tale. It's not that I don't like to listen to John's stories, but this particular one was a bit of a stretch, even for John.

"The truth of the matter was that my ancestor General A. John ("General" was really his first name.) was the first owner of that land down in what they call Flat Rock on accounta all the big flat rocks scattered around. G. A., as we call him, had already settled on the land and had built a cabin there. When the revolutionary war broke out, G. A. tried to mind his own business, but when them gosh-dang red coated devils started picking fights up in these here mountains, he just had to get hisself in the midst of it. He joined up and got hisself made into a real general. His real claim to glory came in the Battle of Big Hungry. I betcha don't know how Big hungry got its name, do ya? Well, I'll tell ya."

Old John was just getting warmed up to his tale now.

"Them thar red coats was all over the place. They was camped down by the river. They had already stolen all the chickens and cows they could find, and there was no crops on account of it being winter time, and they was real hungry. They called that kinda hungry "big hungry", and named the river after that."

"About that time a mess of mountain boys led by G.A. stumbled onto their camp and a mighty battle commenced. Our boys was outnumbered ten to one, but were making real good accounts of themselves, but woulda had to skedaddle outa there if the Overmountain Men hadn't a-stumbled on the fightin' and helped out a mite. Victory was won, and the Overmountain boys, led by G. A., chased them cowardly red coats all the way down to King's Mountain. It was there when they joined up with some other patriot boys to whip the English and Loyalist forces in the Battle of King's Mountain on October 7, 1780. This was the turning point of the war and George Washington hisself was so grateful that he declared that G. A. would receive the land in Flatrock as a reward."

"G.A. and his wife and young-uns lived happily in the old cabin for many years, but as time passed, rich folks from down Charleston way encroached onto the land and built big houses all around them. That guy Memminger was one of them folks. By then, G.A.'s oldest son, Beauregard was living in the old cabin. It was then that the Great War for Southern Independence broke out.

Beauregard immediately joined in the Southern cause and distinguished himself when he and a bunch of other loyal southern boys whipped the dang yankees, which were led by Gen. George Stoneman, in the Second Battle of Big hungry."

John stopped here, got a thoughtful look, scratched his head, and said, "I betcha never read about that particular battle in your school books, didya young-un."

I allowed that I hadn't, to which He replied, "That's 'cause the dang yankees were so embarrassed by losing that partic'lar battle that they hushed it up so no one ever knew that it had even happened. But that's the reason Stoneman passed on through and didn't never establish no fort here like he had planned!"

By now it was time to refill his pipe, so old John did just that, lit it up, and took up his narrative where he had left off. "Ya may not never have heard about that conflict, but Good Old Jefferson Davis did, and he declared that Beauregard should be allowed to stay on his little patch of ground forever, and that he and Memminger should be good neighbors. But now Beauregard and his growing family had about made up their minds to move out anyway to get away from all the crowding in town on account of them dang Yankees and rich Charleston folks moving in and fencing everything in sight."

Apple John finished up by telling me that that was how his ancestors had come to live in the World's Edge community. Then he stood up, stretched, stuck his pipe in the top front pocket of his old bib overalls, called Dog and declared that it was time to amble on back to his old homestead for a good night's rest, promising to tell more the real stories of Hendersonville's early days some other time.

8. APPLE JOHN AND THE LOST COLONY
(Another Nearly-Lost Apple John Story)

Maybe y'all might remember where I talked with my old friend, Apple John, about local history. And John told me about how the recorded history is not quite how things really happened. I have related these facts in my story, *Apple John Rewrites History*. We are fortunate that John's ancestors have been around here long enough to have seen history being made. Not only that, but they have passed the knowledge down through succeeding generations until finally it all rests in John's fertile mind.

The other day I got to wondering just how long John's family has actually resided In the Hendersonville area. The only way to know would be to ask him. John has no phone or other means to reach him, so I had to make my way up to his little cabin way back in the most remote part of the area we know as Worlds Edge. I drove up last Wednesday morning. It was a beautiful Appalachian spring day. Temperature in the upper 60s, Carolina blue sky, and a gentle breeze rustling the leaves that had recently sprung out on the trees. The road ends about a half mile from John's place, so I had to park and hike the rest of the way in. I was thankful that it was such a nice day. When I got to his old cabin, I found my friend resting on his porch in his rickety old rocking chair that his grandpappy had made back when John was just a young-un. As is his habit, John was puffing on his old briar pipe. He grows the tobacco, he calls it "baccer", in a little patch behind the cabin. The pocket on the ragged old flannel shirt that he always wears is stained from carrying the loose tobacco in it. The tobacco juice drips onto his full, white beard, too. The day of my visit, his beard was clean, which is pretty rare. Apparently, he must have washed it as he occasionally does when the stain gets dark and crusty enough to bother him. I let out a "howdy" as I approached as I didn't want to startle him and maybe cause him to tip over backward in his chair.

He replied loudly, "Howdy young-un" as his dog, cleverly named "Dog", let out a series of drawn-out barks. Kind of a combination between bark and howl. As I walked up, John continued, "Come set yerself on that old apple crate over there and tell me all about what's happnin' down in town. Haven't been there in coon's age."

After our usual pleasantries and a short report on the news from town, I got right to the point of my visit. "John, I know your family has been here for a mighty long time, but you've never told me how they first came to settle here."

Old John got a thoughtful look on his wizened old face, spat a load of tobacco juice over the porch railing into the wild flowers below, scratched the seat of his coveralls, and replied. "Well, I'm agona have to give that some thought." At that point he knocked his pipe against the log wall behind him and the ashes floated down to add to the pile already there on the floor boards. Then he proceeded to pull another wad out of his pocket and reload the bowl of his pipe. All of this amid little grumps and snorts. Finally, he lit up the fresh load in the pipe and drawled, "young-un, that's a long story, but if you'll be patient, I'll try to recollect what my old pappy told me about that very subject. As I recall, it was about this time of year back in 1720 that my folks first found their way here."

I should let you know that John may be old as dirt, but his memory for details is unbelievable. He can relate dates, names, and happenings in history in great detail. John continued, "I'd better relate to ya a short history lesson first. Maybe you recall how one of my ancestors discovered how to make Vienna Sausage? And that he was a member of a pirate crew that shipwrecked on the coast of North Carolina and they were searchin' for somethin' to eat while they repaired their boat?"

My readers will recall that story from my research paper *The True History of Vienna Sausage*. John continued, "Well, I left out the part about how some of the men had decided to accept Governor Eden's pardon for previous acts of piracy if they would swear to never repeat them."

I exclaimed. "No, you never told me that. What did these men do after that?"

"I'm gettin' to that right now if you'll jest be patient. It was about this same time that the notorious pirate Captain Blackbeard was trapped down at Ocracoke by Lieutenant Maynard and his men. What pirates weren't killed in the battle, or hanged later, were anxious to get as far away as they could to escape being hung and buried below the low tide line. There was another batch of cut-throats that had been part of the pirate fleet that was with Blackbeard when he ran the *Queen Anne's Revenge* aground at Beaufort."

At this point in John's recitation of my history lesson, the old dog rolled over and John leaned down to rub the belly that was presented to him just for this very purpose. After a few minutes, John took up where he left off.

The Q.A.R. was the ship that Blackbeard captured the year before and was the "flagship" of his pirate fleet. He had hundreds of pirates and several ships at the time. The story goes that he didn't want to share his booty with them all, so he purposely grounded the Q.A.R. on a sandbar and abandoned it. Leavin' it and most of the pirates behind, the captain sailed the sloop Adventure with only a few of his most trusted crew to Ocracoke where Lieutenant Maynard soon cornered him and killed him and most of his crew."

Continuing, John related as how the few pirates that survived joined those that Captain Blackbeard had left behind when he abandoned the Q.A.R., and began looking for a place where they could settle and be safe. As luck would have it, they met up with the pirates that had been pardoned by the governor, and joined with them. After consulting with each other, it was decided that they would head inland towards the mountains.

"Are ya still with me, young-un?", asked John. I guess maybe I had begun to nod off a bit at this point of the story. "Let's get us some nice cold Real Southern Sweet Tea before I tell ya the rest of the story."

As I stood up and stretched my sore muscles, John went around the corner of his cabin to the spring that was the very reason that the cabin had been built on this particular location. There was an old spring house that some ancestor had built there to keep things cool. John has no electricity. The power lines don't come anywhere near John's place, and he wouldn't have power if it was available. He says that if he would let them come in with power lines, it would be the first step in losing his independence. But that's another story. Let's just say that Old Apple John is a bit old fashioned and set in his ways.

Finally, we sat back down and, and after stoking up the old pipe again, he continued. "Here is where we get to how my ancestors came to this ridge in Worlds Edge above what folks now call Chimley Rock." John stood up and pointed vaguely off towards the east. "If you'll wade back into the trees over that-a-way, you'll find all that remains of a village. Nothin' left now but a few foundation stones, and a crumbling chimley here and there. And iffen ya know just where to look, there's a little graveyard."

At this point, John sat back down, pulled the rag from the back pocket of his old coveralls that he wears year-round, wiped the tobacco juice off his face, stuffed the dirty rag back in his pocket, and continued. "I ain't never told no one this, but I'm gonna tell you now. Mebbe you remember Mr. Frank Fitzsimmons book we were a-talkin' about last time we got together?" I said, "Yes, I remember that."

"Do ya recall where he mentioned the other lost colony? Not the one over where Virginia Dare came from, but the one up here in these here mountains? Well, after the pirates had climbed all the way up Chimley Rock, and over the ridge, they were plumb tuckered out. They were so tired that they just plunked their stuff down right where they was standin', and after resting a bit, they built their village right on that very spot. And they didn't call it no lost colony either. They called it *John's Town*. There used to be a soapstone rock next to the trail leading into the community with the name of the village carved into it, but the inscription has worn away over the years, so no one recalls it no more."

John, how did they decide to call it John's Town?"

John took another puff on his pipe, spat again over the rail, and continued, "The pirates got to arguing amongst themselves over which of them the community should be named for. It was soon suggested that they draw straws, and whoever drew the shortest straw could choose the name. The pirate named John won. And it was him that was my great, great, I don't rightly recollect how many greats, grandpappy!"

I had one more question for my friend. "John, where did the women come from that helped the men settle the colony"?

John got one of his inscrutable looks and replied. "That's the part that no one tells ya. There was lots of wild women back in them days that joined-up with the pirate crews. To be accepted, they had to dress like men so's no one would know they was women. They kept up their deception until the cabins were built, then they revealed themselves. By then the men had been so long without female companionship that they welcomed the girls with open arms!"

With that, John let out a loud guffaw, slapped himself on the leg, and finished with, "Now ya know all about my first ancestors in these here mountains. Every word is true!"

I've never known John to be wrong or tell a lie, so I'll leave it to you, my reader, to decide for yourself if what he related to me that day really is the truth.

9. HOW APPLE JOHN GOT HIS NAME
(Another Well-Named Apple John Story)

The other day, I made my regular trip up to Apple John's little home in Worlds Edge. I try to get up to see him every week or two. This time I found him working in the little crab apple orchard behind his cabin. He was spraying the trees with a homemade sprayer. As you know, John has no power up there, including a tractor. John has never even had a car, at least in all the years that I have known him. He thinks that anything like that would make him too dependent on the government somehow.

It may interest you to know how he is able to spray the trees without a tractor and agricultural sprayer. You may recall how I told you about John's time in the Viet Nam War, and how he was an aircraft mechanic on a piper cub aircraft carrier. Well, after the war, John returned to his home near Hendersonville, bringing with him a surplus Piper Cub engine just in case he might find a use for it one day. Well, he did. He mounted it on an old wagon pulled by his faithful mule, cleverly named "Mule", and uses it to spray the insecticide, fertilizer, or whatever. He has a bucket mounted behind the propeller that drips the liquid into the airstream, immediately atomizing it and spraying it out behind.

As I walked up, I realized that John has never told me why he is always referred to as "Apple John." I do know where his family name of John comes from. For those of you that don't know that story, I'll relate a little about it right here.

John's family name can be traced back to when his pirate ancestors settled above Chimney Rock in in the area now called World's Edge. The community was named by John's distant ancestor. He chose *John's Town*, after his own name, John. For those of you that would like to know the complete story on who he was, and how he came to reside in our area, you can refer to my story, *Apple John and the Lost Colony*. That is what we call the remains of the little settlement now that the real name has long been forgotten.

But that doesn't explain the "Apple" part. I knew I'd never find out without asking, so as I walked up, I resolved to do that very thing.

As I approach, I always holler out so he would know that I am coming. "Hey John, how ya doin?" Way back when I first met John, I walked up close to him and startled him. He stumbled and fell, cussing me out as he fell, so I always announce myself. For some reason that I don't understand, he is not startled when I holler out from a distance.

John gave a little wave, walked back to the sprayer, shut the engine off, and replied, "Hey young-un. What'cha doin?"

I jumped right in with my question, "John, how did you come to be known as APPLE John?"

John got a little crooked grin on his wrinkled old face and replied, "C'mon over and set a spell and I'll tell ya all about it."

We sat ourselves down on the old fence that circled the little orchard to keep the deer out, and I waited as John went through his ritual in preparation of taking up his end of the conversation. First, he pulled a stained rag out of the back pocket of his ragged old coveralls and blew his nose on it, then he turned it around and wiped the sweat from his forehead and beard, then stuffed it back in its pocket. Next, he pulled his old pipe from the top coverall pocket, filled it from the stash of "baccer" he keeps in his flannel shirt pocket, and amidst much snorting and puffing, succeeded in getting it lit.   As John had been going through his performance, I had asked, "Is it because you always have an apple in your pocket and are eating them all the time?"

Finally, he proceeded to get on with his answer. "Well, I tell ya, that ain't it a-tall. Do ya remember the story of Johnny Appleseed? And how he travelled around the country planting seeds?"

I said, "Yes, but that was back in the eighteen hundreds, so It couldn't have been about you. Was he one of your ancestors?"

"Nope, that ain't it...exactly. But it was kinda like that. As a matter of fact, the Johnny Appleseed story came about from my relative. My great-great-great, dang, I dunno how many greats there was, was the one who began the apple orchards around these here parts. It was kinda by accident, though. He liked to wander all over and always took apples with him everywhere he went. When it came time for a snack, he's just sit hisself down to eat an apple or two, and spit the seeds out on the ground. Those seeds would spring up, and begin an orchard."

"Awww, John, what did that have to do with the real Johnny Appleseed?"

"Well, it happened this-a-way. My ancestor was the first to be called 'Apple John'. He lived at the same time that this other feller began spreading seeds up in them thar yankee states. Somehow folks connected the two together, but got the name confused a mite, and started calling the other one 'Johnny Appleseed'."

"But John, where did your relative get the apples he carried with him?"

John just shook his head, furrowed his bushy brows, looked me in the eye, and replied. "I 'spect you shoulda known without me spellin' it all out for ya, but you young-uns have to have everything explained to ya. I don't know what's wrong with kids today."

Sometimes old John gets that way. I've found that it's best to just sit quietly and wait for him to settle down. John took his pocket knife out of his pocket, and mumbling to himself, proceeded to clean the ashes out of his corn cob pipe. He has a rather large collection of pipes, some of which belonged to his long line of ancestors going all the way back to the pirate, John. Finally, he struck a match on the backside of his coveralls and lit up. I had to chuckle to myself. He's just about worn a hole through the coveralls at that point. Then he said, "When the pirates were making their way up from the coast, John happened to pick up an apple somewhere. It was so good that he got hisself a supply and carried them with him. When they settled here, he started this very orchard. The first one in these here mountains."

After a few moments, John took up the conversation again. "Ya remember the story of Adam and Eve in the garden? And how Eve picked an apple from the tree of the knowledge of good and evil?" To this I answered, "Yes, but the Bible doesn't actually say 'apple'. It could have been any kind of fruit."

"HA!", John replied with a laugh. "That's where you're wrong! All these newfangled Bible translations are wrong! If ya go to the first, only accurate one, you'll see that it really WAS an apple. You hafta do your reading from that one. The *Authorized Southern King James Bible*."

I wasn't about to argue the point with John. Nor did I point out that there were no known copies left of that particular version after the Yankees had destroyed them all during the Civil War. He had told me once that his church, the *Second Big Hungry Foot Stompin Snake Handling Church,* had saved a copy from the invaders, but I've never seen it.

John picked up again, "And I can't believe that that Adam was any ancestor of mine. Taking an apple from some dang woman that believed anything some old snake told her! Neither of them ain't no relatives of mine!"

I didn't argue the point with him that we all are descended from Adam and Eve. I knew that John would have an answer for that, too.

10. APPLE JOHN AND THE OLD HAG
(Another Terrifying Apple John Story)

Yesterday I made my way to my friend Apple John's old cabin down in the Worlds Edge area of Henderson County. John has made me promise not to tell any more than that about where it is located. I will tell you that it is a chore getting there. The road stops quite a distance away, and I have to hike the rest of the way. I always try to choose a nice day for my visits, and his day was no exception. It is fall and most of the leaves have turned brown and fallen, but that lets me have a view of Lake Lure that is blocked during the rest of the year. It's been a busy fall and I've not been up to see him in a while.

Usually, I find old John out on his porch, or working around outside, but this time, he's nowhere in sight. I call out and am rewarded by a feeble, warbly, "I'm in here young-un." That's not like my friend at all. He always hollers out to the top of his lungs. I wonder if he's hurt or sick and so I hurry in to see. I find him curled up in his bed on his mattress that's stuffed with sugar cane leaves. I can tell he's still in his raggedy old long johns that he sleeps in. His old quilt is pulled up tightly under his chin. He has kind of a wild look in his eyes and he's trembling.

"What's wrong John, I've never seen you like this? You never stay in bed this late."

"I've got me a haint!" John exclaimed loudly. "It done sat on me last night! I couldn't move! It was trying to kiss me! It was AWEFUL!"

"What on earth are you talkin' about?" I asked him. "What's a 'haint' anyway?"

"Don't you young-uns know nothin'? Every soul knows what a haint is."

"No John, I don't know. Tell me. And why are you so afraid?" I asked.

"Dang it---a haint is a haint! A demon! A ghost!" He shouted this out amidst much sputtering and snorting.

"A ghost? There's no such thing as ghosts. You were just dreaming." I replied.

"NO-NO-NO! It warn't no dang dream! It was a HAINT!" (John didn't actually say 'dang', but I don't want to offend my younger reader.) The longer he protested, the louder he got. He was using words he never would have used under normal circumstances.

"Ok John," I said as soothingly as I could. "Why don't you just tell me what you think you saw? And let me help you sit up."

"NOOOO!" My friend wailed. "It might get me! It might be hidin' under the bed! Look under the bed!"

I figured that if I placated him and looked under the bed, he'd settle down. I squatted down, lifted the mattress, and peeked underneath. "Nothing under here but dust bunnies and some old rotten apple cores." John lives alone except for his old coon hound, Dog. Neither one of them is much of a house keeper. John informed me once that, "If I cain't see no trash, it ain't even there." He said that as he tossed an apple core under the bed as he was lying in now. John was always munching on apples.

With that, John pulled his covers down a bit and in a feeble voice, asked, "Are ya sure?" He was still shaking as he began to tell me what he was afraid of. "I wokened up and couldn't move. I was mortal skeered! I tried to holler for Dog, but nothin' would come out! I could see and hear, but it was like I was paralyzed. There wore a heavy weight on my chest and I couldn't hardly breathe."

With that, he pulled the blanket back up and started whimpering again. His eyes were tightly closed and he began drooling a little. "John, what is it? Is there more?"

I waited as he opened his eyes and looked all around him. Then he continued saying, "That's when I saw the haint. It was sittin' on my chest. It was the awfullest thing I ever saw! I was so terrified."

"What did the haint look like, John?" I inquired.

"It was an old hag! Like a nasty witch lady!" he said.

"An old hag? You mean like an old lady?"

"Yes sir! Sittin' right there on my chest. And sneering at me with a malevolent grin. She was a'tryin to choke me to death!"

I was surprised at that. I didn't know that my friend knew words like 'malevolent'.

Old John continued, "It looked jest like my old mother-in-law! A toothless old hag!"

"But John, you've never been married. You told me so yourself."

"Well, it looked jest like my mother-in-law woulda looked iffin I did hadda ever been married!"

I couldn't help myself. I had to laugh. "John, there's a logical explanation for what happened."

"No there AIN'T!" He replied, "I know what it was----it whar a HAINT!"

With that, he tossed the covers aside and began to get out of bed. "Get outa my way! Go get Mule! I gotta go see the preacher man!"

"John, why? What's the big rush for?"

"I gotta get loosed of this here haint! The preacher can make it go away! He can excerote---excercite---ex—DANG! Get RID of it!"

"Oh, you mean exorcise."

"YEP, THAT'S IT---exercise. I done seen him do it once when I was a young-un." My friend was settling down a bit by now. "Them hills is filled with haints. They even got 'em over at that church, *St. John in the Wilderness* in Flat Rock. I done seen 'em there myself once."

"Aw, c'mon John. There aren't any ghosts. And even if there was such a thing, they wouldn't be in a church", I said.

Yes thar is. Everyone says so. People was buried in the walls and under the floor a long time ago. They done been trapped there. Their spirits couldn't get out so theys just haint the place. And thars an old civil war soldier that wanders around the churchyard playing mournful music on his bugle."

"John," I explained, "in the first place, people don't become ghosts when they die. That's just old stories people make up about things they don't understand. There is no such thing as ghosts."

"But I SEEN 'em! I was over at the church holpin' my granpa clean up back when I was a teen-ager. We was under the floor surrounded by dead folks. I seen the graves. And this haint floated right past my face! I could see right through it! I skedaddled outa thar as fast as I could run, and ain't never gone back!"

"Awww, John, there's always a simple explanation. It was probably just dust you stirred up, and your imagination made you think you saw a ghost."

Poor John just wasn't convinced. "But how about the haint that sat on me last night? I FELT it, and SAW it, and couldn't MOVE! I KNOW it was a haint."

"No John, I know you think it was a ghost, but there is a simple explanation." I admit that I was feeling superior to old John because I'd recently read about this very phenomenon, and I couldn't resist showing off a little as I tried to explain it to him. "Did you ever hear of "Occam's razor?" I knew that he hadn't, but as I said, I was showing off. "Occam's razor is the name of a rule that says that the simplest explanation is probably the right one."

"Will that kinda razor kill a haint?" John inquired.

"No John, it's not that kind of razor. It just means that if you have different ideas about how to solve something, the simplest one is usually the best one. Just listen to me while I explain what really happened to you".

I waited to see if my friend would be patient long enough to tell him what had happened. "It just happened that I read about your kind of experience in a medical magazine the other day while I was waiting for a doctor's appointment."

"I don't care! Ya ain't aggona change my mind none." He said menacingly.

I continued anyway. "What you experienced is just a condition that sometimes happens when you sleep. Your brain immobilizes your body while you are dreaming so you won't get up and act out your dreams. You normally don't wake up while it is immobilized, but in rare cases you do. You can see, hear, and think, but you can't move. Your mind imagines that something is holding you down. Often it imagines an old woman. As a matter of fact, the experience is sometimes called the "old hag syndrome".

"That don't prove NOTHIN!" My friend exclaimed. "I jest remembered somethin'. Now I know what it was! It was one of them moon eyed people from over in Hickory Nut Gorge!"

"You mean the old ones that the Cherokee people claimed were here before them? The race of little people with big eyes that were supposed to live over around the Gorge and haunted the first Cherokee to move into the area because they didn't want to share their home land with them? That's just an old Indian legend."

"No, it ain't!" John hollered agitatedly. "It was one of them Moony people just tryin' to haint me!"

"But John, you keep changing your story. First you said it was an old hag, a witch lady. Then it was your mother-in-law. Now it was the moon eyed people. It was just a dream."

"NOOOO! I know what I know! I felt it! You waren't here—you don't know!" By now old John was scooting around on the bed and bouncing violently he was so worked up and hysterical.

It was at that point that I noticed something moving eerily under the bed covers. I almost started to believe my friend really had a haunt when something poked out from underneath the quilt. Slowly the apparition wormed its way out. First a nose, then a big hairy paw, then the rest of John's big old hound dog. Suddenly I understood. Old Dog had been snuggling up to his master and had crawled up on his chest to get warm and was lovingly licking him in appreciation.

11. APPLE JOHN AND THE REVIVAL
(Another Revived Apple John Story)

After church last Sunday I went up to see my old friend Apple John who lives out at World's Edge. It was a hot spring day and I was worn out after hiking in to his cabin. The road ends a half mile before his place, and the trail is up hill and strewn with rocks that I have to scramble over. I hollered out to let John know I was coming, and he answered with his usual "Howdy young-un." After our introductions and small talk, mostly about the morning's church services at his and my churches, John, as usual got to talking about the many revivals he'd experienced. I had been wondering why John was so interested in revival so I asked him about it.

"John, how did you get so interested in church revival, and when did you experience your first one?"

"Well, young-un, that's a mighty interestin' story. Make yerself comfortable while I get ya some refreshin' Southern sweet tea. I jest brewed up a batch this morning. Been coolin' it off in the spring house."

I love the tea that John makes. I've always loved real Southern sweet tea, and John makes it the old-fashioned way and it is the best I've ever tasted. As a matter of fact, John supplied me with some of the history of how Southern sweet tea had come about. I used his information in my scientific report titled *Real Southern Sweet Tea*.

After my friend got himself situated in his old worn-out recliner, he began to relate his tale. "It's like this. It was back In June of 1955. I was jest a sprout in them days, and didn't much care for church. We have always attended the church my great-great-bunch of greats ago, Uncle Beauregard started, the *Second Big Hungry Snake Handlin Foot Stompin Church*. As ya know, the *First Big Hungry Snake Handlin Foot Stompin Church* had been founded by my ancestors at the same time as they settled John's Town up above Chimney Rock way back in the

1700s. That church had begun to get away from the true Gospel; even went to some new-fangled version of God's word. We know that the only true version is the *Authorized Southern King James Bible.*"

At this, John was squirming around and scratching himself. I've noticed before how he does that when he gets excited about his subject. I just sat quietly as he pulled an old Meerschaum pipe from his shirt pocket, and with much huffing and snorting, packed the bowl with a wad of his home grown baccer and lit it. Then, with a sigh, he continued.

"I was slouchin' on the back pew not paying any attention and whittlin' me a new corn cob pipe. My old coon hound, 'Dog', was curled up under the pew snorin' softly at the same time that he kept one eye open just in case somethin' interestin' should happen. Dog always came to church with me. Our preacher was gone on a holy fishin' retreat down offa the mountain with some of his preacher buddies, and Deacon Ebenezer was fillin' in for him. Now old Deacon Eb, as we kids called him, was just getting' wound up real good. He always got real active-like when he preached. Figured it would keep the old ones from fallin' asleep. He was a-hollerin' and jumpin' from pew to pew and wavin' a snake around over his head and sayin' in a loud voice, 'This here snake cain't hurt y'all none if ya believe hard enough! If ya believe, gimme an 'a-man' and stomp yer feet."

At this point, I interrupted my friend with a question. "But John, I thought your church just had the snake part in its name because of the verse in the Bible about handling snakes. Isn't it Mark 16:17-18 where it says, 'These signs will accompany those who believe: In my name they will . . . pick up snakes with their hands.' What kind of snake was it?"

"It was a king snake.", John answered.

To that I asked, "But John, king snakes aren't poisonous." Why don't you use something like a rattlesnake or copperhead?"

John shook his head and squinted at me like he does when he thinks I should know better than to ask such a silly question. Then he explained, "The Southern King James says, 'Y'all shan't tempt the Lord, but testin' him out is good for ye spirit.' What this means is that ya shouldn't temp God enough to make him mad at ya, but it's good to build your faith if ya jest tease him a mite. A buzz-tail would be too much of a temptation for the good Lord."

I'd better explain right here that "Buzz-tail" is what John calls a rattlesnake.

Old John paused in his recitation and relit the pipe which had gone out. Presently he took up again. "Deacon had finished his sermon finally after talking for only an hour and a half, and the choir had begun singin' our closin' hymn from the old blue hymnal, the one with shaped notes that even folks that cain't read real notes could figure out. It was right as the sopranos reached the highest point in their performance that Dog spied a lizard scurrying under the pews. He took off after it, and as he did, he crawled between Miss Bessie's legs. She let out an ear-splittin' screech as she leaped onto the pew behind her, tossin' her hymnal high inta the air. Whooda known that such an old lady could move that fast!

At this point in his narrative, John jumped up and began waving his hands around as he continued, "Dog was howlin' and soundin' like a demon straight outa Hell! Right away, everyone else joined in as the spirit moved them. Men commenced speakin' in tongues and rollin' on the floor. The women folk swooned and fell-out all around the church. Ya shoulda seen it! A bunch of folks rushed up to the alter hollerin', 'I believe---I wanna be saved!' Men and women alike was weepin' and callin' on the Lord. It was right then that God revealed to me that I was a sinner and needed to trust Jesus, so I ran up to the alter, too. Even deacon Eb dropped to the floor and gave his life to Jesus for the first time.

Wow John, I exclaimed. "That must have been a sight to behold."

"Sure was! After a bit, things settled down and the newly sanctified folks all began askin' each other, 'what are we agonna do now?' It was decided right then and there that we would all go down to the Big Hungry River and get us baptized. Deacon Eb allowed as that would be a good thing in the sight of the Lord, so we proceeded to do that very thing. We all took turns cheerin' as Deacon Eb dunked each one of us under the cold, clear water, and held us 'til we bubbled. He believed in being thorough by giving us time to be washed clean of our sins. Even Dog jumped in and was saved. Then we all headed back to the church and had us a big dinner of sweet tea and Southern fried chicken. That's the way for new Christian folks to finish up a good revival!

With that, John sat back down and finished with, "That's why I'm so excited about church revivals."

"Hey John, whatever happened to the snake?"

"Well young-un, all God's creatures bow down before King Jesus, even the king snake!"

(*Postscript to my readers:* The way John relates this drama, it would appear that it is baptism that saves a person, but that is not how it happens. John knows that you are saved at the moment that you confess your sins and trust in Jesus Christ alone for the free gift of eternal life.)

12. APPLE JOHN – FIREMAN?
(Another Firey Apple John Story)

I made my regular trip up to my good friend, Apple John's house yesterday. It was a hot day and the last half mile climb on the dusty dirt trail had left me sweaty and dirty. As I got to John's cabin, I could hear splashing in the creek behind his house. When I went around the corner of his cabin, I could tell that he was taking a bath in the creek. That was a real surprise as John rarely bathes, especially on a week day, and this was Tuesday. I hollered out as I approached. "Hey John, what are you doing getting a bath this time of week?"

"Hiya young-un!" He replied in his high pitched, scratchy voice. "I Jest got back from a fire and I was all covered with ashes and smokey smellin'."

"Fire?" I exclaimed. "What fire? I haven't heard of any fire."

John peered out from under his wooly eye brows as he grabbed an old torn rag off of a bush next to the creek and as he commenced drying himself off, he said, "Did I ever tell ya that I'm a real, regulation volunteer fire fighter?"

"No John, I had no idea!" I remarked. "How long have you been fighting fires? I didn't even know there was a fire department anywhere around here in."

"Well set yerself here in the shade," my friend said as he pulled on his ragged flannel shirt that he wears every day, winter or summer, and his tattered, stained coveralls. He then pulled out a long stemmed "Canadian" pipe from a pile of pipes on the apple crate next to his chair. He likes to vary his pipes, and it seems he has a different one every time I see him. He pulled a wad of his home grown baccer, that's what he calls his tobacco, from the stained shirt pocket and proceeded to poke it into the pipe's bowl with the little finger of his left hand. He struck a match on the seat of his coveralls, and amidst puffing and snorting, got it going to his satisfaction before starting into his story.

"It's like this; the men-folk in my family have been fightin' fires for several generations. We are all members down at the Big Hungry *Foot Stompin Snake Handlin Church* and volunteer fire department. We keep all of our equipment in an old barn there. My great-great-great granpappy started the fire department, and was the first chief. Now, my aunt's biggest son, R. I. Diculus, is the chief. The kids in the church take turns ringin' the bell when the news of a fire comes in. No matter what the bell-ringin' is for, we always scurry to gather.

John snuffled and spat a wad of baccer juice before continuing, "We have us a fire tower right behind the church. Always someone up thar a-watchin' for smoke. That's how we knows there's a fire. Soon's the tower guy sees smoke; he hollers for the bell boy to yank on the rope to set the bell a-ringin'! Great fun for a young boy!"

To that I asked, "But John, how to you guys afford the fancy fire engines and other equipment?"

"Equipment? Fancy?" John exclaimed. "We don't need no new-fangled fancy equipment!" We've got the same equipment we've always had. Iffen it was good enough for old great grandpappy, it's good enough for us! We have the same stuff that my old relatives bought with some of their share of pirate loot that they brought up here to the mountains with them."

For those of you that don't know, John's ancestors were pirates that had left the trade and come here back in the 1700s, but that's another story.

My old friend started in again, "I'm agonna relate to you about that very same equipment, but first, I'm powerful thirsty. Sit tight as I git us some good old real Southern sweet tea from the spring house."

When he returned and gave me my tea, he slouched back down in the old broken-down recliner he had reclaimed from the roadside where someone had dumped it, then he took a long slurp of his tea, belched, and began where he had left off. "Everything we have has been passed from one generation to the next. Well, that ain't exactly true, the critters are different, but there're descended from the first ones."

"Our biggest engine is our hook and ladder wagon, but we don't hardly never need us the ladder—no cabins over a story tall with a loft here-a-bout. It's pulled by a team of four oxen, and takes two men and a boy to drive. One man sets up front and drives the front half, and the other is in the hind end steerin' the back wheels. The boy runs ahead skeerin' the chickens outa the way."

By now it was time for John to knock the ashes out of his pipe. Then go through the routine of filling and lighting it again. I noticed that there was a piece of rag wrapped around the stem. "What's the rag for John?" I asked. "Well, I tell ya. I done broke the stem this mornin' and had to glue it back together. I had to tear a piece off my hanky to wrap around it while the goop dries. Bakker juice mixed with a bit of apple seed chewins makes a mighty fine glue, doncha know!"

When he was satisfied that the pipe was going good, he said, "Another ve-hickle that we have is a mule drawn tanker wagon piled high with empty glass moonshine jugs that we fill with water from the river. We-uns used to have a big oaken tank on the wagon, but it rotted out years ago. Best place to fill the jugs on the water wagon is in the river right next to the skinny-dipping beach at the *Sunny Bottom* nudist camp. But don't worry yerself none about that, Chief Diculus makes the guys pull flour sacks over their heads before going down to fill the water jugs so they don't see nothin' they shouldn't."

My friend was really into his story now. He jumped up exclaiming, "Ya wanna see my fireman's suit?"

"Sure John, I'd like to see your uniform."

With that, he ran into the cabin and I could hear him rummaging around mumbling to himself. Soon he emerged in his attire. I'll do my best to describe it all to you. Rather than the uniform I expected, he had on another set of farmer's bib coveralls. This was an old pair that was worn out and had many holes in it, through which showed his long, pink underwear he always wears. It was caked with a thick layer of what looked like mud. It was thick and cracked, but thoroughly covered the fabric of his coveralls. When I asked, John explained that it was special mud from a clay pit nearby that acted like a fire proof coating. I noticed that he wore the same worn-out flannel shirt that he wears all the time.

For a helmet, he had the top shell from a big river cooter. He had spray painted the shell red. I'd

better explain just what a cooter is. Folks around here call most all water turtles, "cooters", except for the snapping turtle, which they call mud turtles. Land turtles are sometimes called box turtles, which is what they are, or terrapins, which they aren't. The particular shell that John was wearing was from what really is named a "river cooter". Eastern river cooter to be exact. The shell was tied to his head with a piece of rope. But I see that I've gotten away from our story.

I was surprised to see that he had on his best Sunday boots. When asked, my friend explained that they hardly had any holes in the soles. He didn't want to burn his feet on hot coals. As usual, he had no socks on. He claims that socks are too confining and cut off his "cir-e-lation".

After I had a chance to admire his "fireman suit", John went back in the cabin and changed. He soon came back and resumed his position in the recliner, and continued telling me about the fire department.

"We even got us a fire dog. He's a special-bred coon hound with big black spots. Old Sparkletail. He got that name when his tail caught on fire when he was jest a pup. When he howls, he sounds jest like a real si-reen!" With that, John let out a piercing howl in imitation of the old hound. As soon as he did that, his own dog, named "Dog", took up the cry. Immediately, hounds all over the county joined in! Then the coyote pack that's always foraging around hoping to catch a free-range chicken added to the cacophony! That apparently tickled my friend and he broke down into a series of guffaws interrupted by bouts of coughing. Eventually, the dogs, coyotes, and John wound down, and with a sheepish grin, he went on.

"We got us a first responder too. Chief Diculus's son has the only horse way out here beyond World's Edge, so he got the job. Cain't none of the rest of us get there that fast. We all jest shows up when we can."

"Where was the fire today, John?"

"Warn't no fire," he answered. "Miss Bessie's cat had been chasing a squirrel up a tree and it got skeered and wouldn't come down."

"But John, how'd ya get all messed up if there wasn't a fire?" I asked.

"Don't ya know nothin', young-un?" John said in a grumpy voice. "How do ya think we'd know about the cat if Miss Bessy hadn't lit a signal fire?" John shook his head and stuck his bony finger in my face. "You dang young folks jest don't think! Trouble was, the pile of brush she lit up to call us was piled next to her barn, and it caught the barn on fire. We had to put that out before we could get her dang cat outa the tree. Cain't figure why the dang woman would light a fire up against the barn, no how."

"Hey John, does everyone always go to every fire call?"

"Dang tootin'! We always have us a big feast after every call. Granny John always has big pitchers of real Southern sweet tea ready. And most of us Southern fellers is great cooks."

"But, where do y'all get the food to cook?"

"We're always careful to stop and scoop up road kill on the way to answer a call. A feller can work up a powerful appetite fightin' a fire. We always have us a good eat before heading home. Fried Possum, squirrel-on-a stick, toad smash, and best of all, if we hit us a deer, we can feast on barbecue deer steaks! But my favorite is real Southern deep fried snake nuggets! Don't matter what kind, they-ums all good nuggets! Iffen it's durin' the winter, and we don't get us no road kill,

Granny cooks us up some real Southern fried chicken. Dang pesky chickens are all over the place, and no one would miss a few."

I suppose that's why it's called the "Big Hungry" fire department.

13. APPLE JOHN AND THE FRUIT OF THE VINE
(Another Tasty Apple John story)

My old friend, Apple John stopped by the other day to invite me down to his church for their annual "Stompin' Festival". His church, the *Second Big Hungry Foot Stompin', Snake Handling Church* has been holding these festivals for as far back as anyone can remember. I look forward every year to these special events. I'd better explain that this church is steeped in tradition going all the way back to the first settlers in the Appalachian Mountains. I'll try to explain their strange ways as we go.

"Hey Young-un!" John always calls me "young-un" even though I'm almost as old as he is. "Ya ready for a powerful lot of fun?"

"Yep", I exclaim. "I remember last year. You folks sure know how to make worship fun!"

At this, my friend grinned one of his face splitting grins, let out a chortle, and slapped himself on the seat of his old, ragged coveralls. "Then c'mon. We're agonna have more fun that a frog flickin' flies."

I had no idea what that meant, but obviously it had great meaning to him. I asked him once what he meant with these bizarre descriptions. He got a puzzled look on his face, spat a stream of baccer juice at an ant hill, and said, "I jest say 'em, I don't explain 'em."

I climbed up beside John in his old wagon that he always brought into town. He refuses to learn how to drive a car. I even offered to give him my old one when I bought myself a new one, but he got a disdainful look, and stated, "I ain't never gonna get me one of them infernal things. They be of the Devil!", and that was the end of it. "Get a-movin, Mule!" That's what John calls the broken down mule that pulls his wagon. He also has a dog named "Dog", but Dog isn't allowed to go the festival. He tends to want to jump in the barrels when the grapes are being smashed, and chase the snakes during the snake handling service later in the day.

John just says, "Stay Dog." and his faithful old hound dog slowly lifts himself up and drags himself under a nearby bush where he immediately goes back to sleep.

The pastor of John's church always combines their annual foot washing ceremony with a grape stomping event. They time it for when the grapes are ripe. The grapes are a special kind that they have developed over several generations just for their potency. It is as if they have already fermented right on the vine. They have to watch the kids that they don't sneak in amongst the vines and get drunk eating grapes!

John told me that the vines are extra-blessed because an early apostle of their denomination had laid hands on the very first vines and blessed them way back in the early days. The juice they produce is used primarily to make their communion wine. They have communion a LOT! The Bible says to do it every time you meet. They take that command VERY seriously!

But communion wine is not the only thing the grapes are used for. They also keep a supply on hand as an antidote for the snake bite in case someone is accidentally bitten during the mid-week snake handling service. They believe that they are protected from the effects of the venom, but only if the believer has enough faith. The wine is strong stuff! Even so, sometimes it takes at least a whole jug to sufficiently counteract the venom.

My friend further explained that the Authorized Southern King James Bible doesn't have anything indicating that drinking alcohol is actually a sin. After all, he explained, when Jesus turned water into wine, they were in the middle of a big bash at the wedding feast and everyone got "Holy snorkled-up" as John puts it. This is one of the chapters they use for their belief in drinking much wine. It is very clear in John two, six. "And there were set there six waterpots of stone, after the manner of the purifying of the Jews, containing two or three firkins apiece for every soul." And in two, ten "And saith unto him, 'Every man at the beginning doth set forth good wine; and when men have well drunk, then that which is worse: but thou hast kept the good wine until now.' Then the ruler of the feast ordered all the people to drink, "It is with the good attitude of thanksgiving that we shall all partake of God's grace and drinketh our fill.'"

Parts of these verses are not in newer versions but make it clear that drinking much wine isn't the problem, it is drinking with a wrong attitude that is sinful.

This is a good time to tell you about the celebration. So, here we go. John will explain parts of it in his own words. I could tell we were getting close by the carefree laughter coming up the trail from the church. By the time we got there at around ten in the morning, they had already been preparing for several hours. They were pretty well "snorkeled up" from sampling last year's product. They like to finish it off before getting into the fresh batch.

The women were busy preparing the fried road kill and all the other fixins for the dinner, while the men got the stomping barrels out of storage. These were old oaken barrels that had been cut in half just for grape stomping, and were well broken in. They were carefully saved from year to year. The kids were in the vineyard collecting the grapes. The teen's job was to inspect last year's wine skins to be sure they were suitable. Most weren't, but the women had been gathering nauga hydes and making new whine skins. It is a carefully guarded secret as to where the naugas are still being bred way back in the Big Hungry somewhere. Early settlers had discovered the naugas many generations ago, and learned that their hides were much better to create wine skins from than the pig bladders that had been used previously.

By now we had come up to the wooden shed behind the church cabin. I could see that my friend was getting excited. "Hurry up, young-un! They's all gotten a head start on us!" He jumped down and went running in his ambling manner over to where the older folks were gathered around the table that contained last year's remains. I notice that the gallon jugs were just about empty. John grabbed one that still had some wine left, flopped down on a bench, flipped the jug up on his shoulder, and took a big gulp.

"Ahhhh, that's smooooth," followed by a long, drawn-out belch.

Just then the pastor came out of the church house and called out, "Hey bretherin and sisterin, it's about time to get started, c'mon in and let's sing us a few songs to get in the mood."

With that, John put down the jug and we all headed into the old rugged log church building. The choir was already singing an old hymn from the shaped-note hymnal. John has a spot on a pew reserved for himself right down in front. We sat down and my friend immediately started tapping his foot and burst out loudly with his raspy voice. A couple of old ladies looked over at him and glared, but he didn't care.

Preacher O. L. Timey, with much ceremony, gets up and climbs the ladder up to his pulpit, smooths down his three-piece coveralls, and beginning his short sermon, reads some scriptures about wine from the ASKJB.

"First Timothy, chapter five, verse twenty-three says 'Drink no longer water, but use much wine for thy stomach's sake and thine often infirmities'".

Preacher Timey comments, "Aren't we poor creatures infirm from birth? And it is in Romans fourteen, twenty-one that we find, 'It is good neither to eat flesh, nor to drink wine, nor any thing whereby thy brother stumbleth, or is offended, or is made weak.' And again in 1 Corinthians 8:13, it tells us 'Wherefore, if meat make my brother to offend, I will eat no flesh while the world standeth, lest I make my brother to offend.'"

"Is Paul saying that we should never eat meat again? Or drink water again? Or that y'all ain't never supposed to do ANYTHING again? Why that ain't it at all! He's just a-sayin' that if yer with a bunch of them dang heathen yankees, then slow it down a bit 'cause they jest don't understand the truth of the word like we-uns do. But when we-uns are all together here, we ain't agonna stumble, are we?"

"I know y'all understand what the good book says in Timothy chapter four, verse four. 'For everything created by God is good, and nothing to be refused, if it be received with thanksgiving, including wine.' Ain't we all thankful for the fruit of the vine that God made so abundantly for us? And ain't we thankful that he taught us how to make the good wine from it?"

The whole time, everyone present is exclaiming "A-man brother!" and "Preach on preacher!"

Then Preacher Timey let out a "Praise de Lawd, y'all! Let's get on with the stompin!"

With that, the preacher started skipping down the aisle, then the deacons, then the choir, then the rest of us row-by-row. Everyone was in high spirits, yelling and singing as we went. We filed out the doors and made our way back to the shed where the barrels had already been filled with grapes. The men hurriedly pulled off their boots and rolled their coveralls and long johns up while the ladies unlaced their high-top shoes and rolled their long dresses up, tucking them into their belts.

John was among the first to get ready and he quickly jumped up and ran over to the first barrel. Soon others followed. Everyone crowded three or four to a barrel. Always men with men, and women with women. Kids that had reached the age of accountability and had been baptized in the spirit had their own smaller barrels.

I didn't know if I would be allowed to help, but my friend hollered out, "C'mon young-un, I got special permission and prayed for ya, so it's right and good that ya join us." I climbed in gingerly with John and waited to see what would happen next. Everyone was standing respectfully, even the kids. Then Preacher Timey threw up his hands and exclaimed, "It's stompin time y'all! Let's sing together that old favorite hymn, *Stompin in the Grapes.*

John explained, "It is tradition that we wait for preacher to start us off, and we always begin with that-there same song."

Everyone circled around in a counterclockwise direction and stomped in time with the music. I hadn't noticed before, but some of the men had fiddles, banjos, or Jews harps, and played with much enthusiasm. As if on cue, every few minutes, we all turned and marched the other direction. Grape juice was flying everywhere, and before long, we all took on a purplish hue. Eventually, as if on cue again, we all stopped and one-by-one, climbed out of the barrels and lined up behind the preacher.

"Hey John," I inquired, "What happens now"?

"Heshup, young-un, you'll see presently."

It was then that I noticed a pond next to the shed with benches circling it. Preacher Timey stepped forward a couple of paces and said in a loud voice, "Bretherin and sisterin, it is now time for the foot washing. Y'all knows what to do."

With that. We all moved to the benches. Half of the folks sat down, and the remainder of them kneeled down in front of the ones sitting. I was one of those on the benches, and old John was in front of me. Preacher Timey stood up from where he had been kneeling and read from the book of John, chapter thirteen. When he got to verse six he turned towards us and said, "Y'all folks sitting say along with me what Peter said, "Then cometh he to Simon Peter, and Peter saith unto him, 'Lord, dost thou wash my feet?'"

"Now all of you-uns kneeling also say along with me, 'Jesus answered and said unto him, What I do thou knowest not now; but thou shalt know hereafter.'"

As the scripture was being recited, those kneeling carried out the action of washing the feet of the ones sitting. They each had a pail of water next to them and soap and a washcloth.

And so it went until we reached verse ten. When we had read that, and everyone that was sitting had had his feet washed, the preacher said, "Switch places y'all." And we did as he asked, and all was done over again. Then Preacher Timey repeated verse ten; J saith to him, he that is washed needeth not save to wash his feet, but is clean every whit: and ye are clean, but not all."

He continued by saying, "Y'all be clean, but not all. Now it's time to clean the rest of our bodies!"

Immediately we all ran into the pond and began splashing ourselves and each other. John leaned over close to me and whispered, "We's all havin' more fun than a hog in a mud hole!"

After a sufficient amount of time to wash the grape juice off, the preacher climbed out and turning toward us, said in a reverent voice. "C'mon y'all. It's time to partake in Holy Communion."

"But John," I asked, "What about the grapes? What happens to the juice now?"

"Doncha worry yerself none about that. The preacher and elders will take care of it presently. It's a carefully guarded secret jest how they make the sanctified wine."

We all marched single file with hands folded and heads bowed, back to our pews in the church. The preacher and deacons were standing behind the alter rail. Some held a tray with waxed paper cups stacked on it, and some had a loaf of bread. The preacher was behind a small table which held a large pitcher of wine and his Bible.

As he opened the Bible and read from Luke, chapter two, the first row of people came forward and stood before the alter rail. When he got to verse nineteen about the bread being Jesus' body, the deacons held out the loaves of bread and each person tore off a piece and put it in his mouth.

Then as he got to verse twenty, he put down his Bible and poured the wine into the cups, and the deacons held out the trays so everyone could take a cup. As he picked his Bible back up and finished reading the verse, everyone lifted the cup to their lips and drank deeply of the wine.

After all had come forward and taken their turn, Preacher Timey served to the deacons, and they served him. He then said a prayer of thanksgiving, and then blessed the entire congregation. After that he quickly descended from the stage and hollered, "Follow me, y'all! It's time to share our meal t'gether. The women folk have put us on a mighty fine spread!"

I followed my friend out to the covered tables on the other side of the church. A couple of boys had stopped in the church entry foyer and grabbed hold of the bell tower ropes that were hanging down and were pulling enthusiastically. I wondered why and asked John about it.

"The ladies all fix dinner in their own kitchens at home before the service and leave it in the oven to keep warm until it's time to eat. The bells mean it's time to bring the fixins to church."

I was amazed at the amount and variety of the food that soon showed up on the tables. The ladies had done a nice job preparing the tables for the meal. John told me that they get together and sew up new table cloths each year. They were made like quilts with different patterns for each table. In the center of each was a large size canning jar filled with flowers. And each table also had a pitcher of real Southern sweet tea prominently displayed. The pitchers were all very old and were family heirlooms. The ladies are proud of their sweet tea and want it displayed in the most inviting manner possible. John told me that they even have a contest each year to see who can make the best tea. Each family has a little plot of tea plants and a source of Florida sugarcane. They even crown a "Miss Southern Sweet Tea" chosen from among the sweetest of the girls of the community. Buzzard wings that had been carefully dried and festooned with brightly covered ribbons hung from the rafters over each table.

The tables were soon filled with Real Southern Delicacies. The first course was "Poke Salat" that was created from the local poke berry plants. For vegetables, there was mashed potatoes smothered in bear fat gravy, a mess of collards flavored with cooter drippings, candied sweet taters loaded with homemade goat milk butter, and some kind of beans I couldn't recognize. Then the main course. There were several varieties of road kill casserole. Possum, coon, and ground hog. Then the inevitable real Southern pan-fried chicken. Each table had a big loaf of craklin' corn bread. There were even some platters of deep-fried chicken feet. Several kinds of pie would be brought for dessert. For now, they were left in the ovens to keep warm.

I almost forgot the most important part! Right in the center of the pavilion was a table, bigger than all the rest, filled with every conceivable pork product. There was pulled pork bar-b-q smothered in Carolina sweet sauce, pork butt, deep fried bacon, hawg jowls, pig-skin rinds, pickled big feet, hog leg drumsticks, link sausage in pig intestine, hot pepper sausage patties, and right in the center was a roasted pig head with the biggest, reddest apple I have ever seen clamped tightly in its mouth! At each end of the table was a bowl filled with sugar coated pig tails.

"Hey John, y'all sure don't waste anything do ya!"

John let out a chortle and laughingly exclaimed, "No sir. We use everything exceptin' the squeak!" Just then a couple of boys ran past blowing on the pig-nose whistles, "Squeek-squeek!"

I wondered why there was no wine since this whole day was planned around the "fruit of the vine." John soon cleared that up for me. "We-uns don't wanna over-do it y'know." I noticed a bit of a slur in his speech as he said that. Between sampling the old wine when we first arrived, sips before and after the grape stomping and foot washing ceremonies, and the cups at communion, he was definitely feeling the effects.

After prayer by the preacher, we settled in for the feast. No one said a word as we plowed in. Nothing to be heard but munching and crunching with an occasional subdued belch. Everyone had prepared by tucking a large cloth napkin under their collars. That was a good thing as grease was flying everywhere. I looked over at John and grease had colored his beard and was dripping off the end onto the napkin. A couple of hours later we had slowed considerably.

But we weren't finished yet. Out came the pies from the various homes. The usual apple pie, cherry pie, pecan pie. John always reminds me that it is pronounced "pee-can", never "pe-cahn". "Only a dang Yankee says pe-cahn" he says. Rhubarb pie, sweet tater pie, chocolate pie. Pear pie, paw-paw pie, strawberry pie. Shoefly pie, peanut butter pie, and of course, banana cream pie.

But then there were some not so usual ones. Vinegar pie, red oak acorn pie, navy bean pie, pork and bean pie. "Stargazy pie" with minnow heads poking out. Hot dog pie made from homemade hot dogs, Twinkle pie, fried green tomato pie. Pickle and peanut butter pie with yogurt, green bean pie, and catfish pie.

I don't see how, but the pies soon disappeared. These folks can really put away the chow! After we were done, and everyone pitched in to clean up, it was time for a short nap. Folks just found a cozy spot on the ground and stretched out. Soon the air was filled with a cacophony of snores. Gentle murmur snores, hit and miss snores, and loud earth rattling snores. I soon drifted off too, but naturally I never snore.

After a while, we all began to wake up. Preacher Timey soon jumped up and said with much enthusiasm, "Now loved-uns, it's time for the next portion of our service: The snake handling ceremony!"

This is the part that everyone had been waiting for! Everyone let out a big whoop and ran back to the church! When we were all inside, the doors were pulled closed and locked. After everyone had taken his or her seat

the preacher said, "Let us now bow our heads and pray for a safe but humbling service.

After the prayer, the deacons went behind the alter and retrieved several large canvas bags and brought them out into the room, spacing themselves every few rows. When they were ready, everyone began counting down, "10-9-8-7-6-5-4-4-2-1" At "0", a loud cheer went up as the sacks were turned upside down and serpents slithered out! There were big ones, small ones, brightly colored ones, black ones, spotted ones, striped ones. I tried to identify them. I saw corn snakes, black snakes, green snakes, garter snakes, water snakes, and many I didn't recognize, but no venomous ones.

"John, I don't understand. Aren't there supposed to be venomous vipers for the service?"

My friend got that sly little grin that he often gets as he explains something to me that he thinks I should already know. He leaned close and whispered, "Mark sixteen, verse eighteen says, 'They shall take serpents; and if they drink any deadly thing, it shall not hurt them; they shall lay hands on the sick, and they shall recover.' But the good book also says, 'Ye shall not tempt the LORD your God.'"

He continued, "It's okay to temp God a bit to show our trust, but we don't wanna temp him TOO much." Then John got a thoughtful look and continued, "Sometimes a cotton mouth gets in here by mistake. And once in a while we's even get us a buzz tail!" That's what John calls a rattle snake.

He went on, "It's easy to see how a cotton mouth could be mixed up with a regular old water snake. They's all look 'bout alike. But a buzz tail is different. Maybe the Devil sneaks him in on us. Sometimes someone isn't trustin' God enough and he gets nipped!"

"Wow John! Does God protect them when that happens?"

To that my friend got that thoughtful look again. "He sure does, but jest to be sure, when that happens, we keeps us a jug of the best wine left over from communion as insurance. It's already been blessed and sanctified, so it's kinda like double-blessed."

Then John chuckled and proclaimed, "Sometimes one of the old-uns will get hisself bitten on purpose jest so's he can get hisself another little sip!"

During this time, everyone was grabbing snakes and holding them up in the air. Some of the men would wrap them around their bodies. A few of the younger women were kissing the snake---on the lips! Most of the kids were standing off to the side just watching and giggling. The old folks were praying loudly and speaking in tongues. This continued for at least an hour. Then the preacher said a final prayer.

He finished by saying, "We've all been mightily blessed. Bretherin and sisterin, can I get an a-man?" And all said, "A-man". Then he concluded with, "I know y'all will help gather up the serpents and return 'em to their bags. As always, help yerselves to as many as y'all want to make your fried snake for supper."

Then as we all left, he added, "don't forget to take a jug with you-uns to wash yer supper down with."

And so ended this year's Stompin' Festival. A great time of blessing was had by all. I'll look forward to next year, but for now, it's time to help my friend up on his old wagon and urge Mule to take us home. We hadn't even begun moving before old John was fast asleep. It's a good thing that Mule knows the way, because I soon joined my friend in slumber.

14. APPLE JOHN LEARNS TO FLY
(Another Airy Apple John Story)

It was an early spring day when I made my way up to my friend's old cabin at World's Edge. As usual, I had to hike in the last mile or so because the ragged pathway was too strewn with rocks and fallen branches to drive my car. As I drew close, I could hear the sound of an engine of some kind. That was unusual in that old John doesn't believe in using power of any kind. I turned the last corner and saw John leaning over what appeared to be an engine mounted on a rickety framework of old discarded lumber. John drags discards like that home with him on his dilapidated wagon on the rare occasions when he travels into town. He looked up as I walked up to him and straightened himself up, calling out, "Hey young-un!" as he shut the engine off.

"What are you doing, John, where did you get that old motor? What is it anyway?"

To this, my friend replied, "Ain't ya never seen this before? I've had it for a mighty long time. I brought it with me from when I came home at the end of the Viet Nam War." I'd forgotten about the old piper Cub engine he had brought home with him after the war.

"I knew that you were in the war, and that you served as an aircraft mechanic on a carrier."

"Shore 'nuff," he exclaimed as he pulled a dirty rag out of the back pocket of his ragged old coveralls that he always wore and started trying to wipe the dirt and grease from his gnarled old hands. "It was the Piper Cub carrier USS Crashalot. They let me have this engine as they were decommissioning the ship. I like to fire her up sometimes when I get to missing the old days."

"I know how proud you are of the time you served. You've told me some stories of your time aboard. And I'm proud of you too. All of you that served our country are real heroes."

With that, old John just shuffled his feet a bit and wiped his nose with the rag leaving a greasy smear. I could see a tear roll down his wizened old cheek as he timidly asked, "Would ya take me down to

Johnson's airfield?"

"Where? I've never heard of it." I asked.

"Oh, I forget you young-uns don't know nothin' about things like that." John snorted. "That's the old name of the airport down in Hendersonville. Jest set yerself down a spell on the porch while I clean myself up a mite."

With that, my friend ambled into his cabin. I busied myself trying to remember what what John had told me about his time in Viet Nam. It wasn't long before I dosed off in John's old rocker. About then I felt a bony hand shaking my shoulder and heard a piercing, "HEY YOUNG-UN wake yerself up! Let's get a move on. The day ain't gettin' no younger!"

I was surprised to see that he had on a white uniform jacket and blue navy tie over his coveralls, along with a white sailor's cap. Most surprising of all was that they were clean. "Wow, John, those are spiffy!"

"Yesirree-bob, I'm right proud of 'em!", he exclaimed with pride. "I put 'em on now and then on special occasions."

We walked quietly down the trail to the car. I could tell that my friend was deep in thought so I

didn't disturb him. I knew he'd say what was on his mind when he was good and ready. We soon arrived at the car and climbed in. I helped John fasten his seat belt. He's suffering from some arthritis after his long life spent toiling around his property in all kinds of weather. After a bit he sat up straighter and began to talk.

"I betcha don't know nothin' about the old airfield. It's been there a long time. Goes back to when Oscar Meyer founded the Hendersonville Airport in 1932. Meyer started the first airport himself. He cleared the cornfield, built a runway, and built the first hangers there. Then years later, Mr. Leland Johnson, who owned land next to the airport called 'Johnson's Airfield', done sold it to the museum for their new hanger in about 1992. That's whar we're agoin' today.

Then my friend got a thoughtful look, then a mischievous grin, and then he said in a quiet, conspiratorial voice, "And here's somethin' else that folks don't know. When Oscar was just a young-un, and beginnin' to build his first flyin' machines, he had a little accident one day. He done hit a hog that was crossin' the airstrip. Kilt it deader'n a possum on a busy highway! Shredded it in the propeller! This was also about the time he was considerin' his future. Right then and there, he scraped up the remains and used it to stuff his first Oscar Meyer wiener!"

Ignoring the part about the possum, I asked, "I didn't know all that. How come you know so much about the old airport?"

John got a faraway look in his eyes and just stared out the window for a moment before saying, "I spent a lot of my early years over there. My uncle Orville used to take me with him when he went on crop dusting jobs. He kept his old Curtis Jenny that he had converted into a crop duster in a hanger there. He used to let me help him work on his plane."

"Is that how you came to learn how to work on airplane engines?" I asked.

"It sho-nuff is!" he exclaimed enthusiastically. "I was young and a-yearnin' for adventure when the war broke out, so it warn't long before I decided to join up. I didn't know nothin' about anything else, but I was a right good at twistin' a wrench, so's I tried to join the air force. They wouldn't take no one that warn't a college graduate, so's I went down to the navy guy and he signed me right up. Said they had a special place for someone like me, and shipped me off to join the good ol' Crashalot. I thought that was jest fine 'cause the guys always laughed at me when we went skinny dippin' down to the swimmin' hole on the Big Hungry 'cause I didn't know how to swim, and I thought I could larn how iffen I joined up in the navy."

"You never told me about how that all came about, or your growing up around airplanes. Did you ever learn to fly one?"

With that, old John reached into his front pocket and pulled out one of the apples he always carries with him for a snack, took a big bite out of it, and after a few chews, proceeded with his story. "Well, young-un, I did try to fly Uncle Orville's Genny a time or two. Old Orv, that's what we kids called him, would get me up good and high, then let go of the stick and take his feet offa the peddles, and say, 'She's all yorn!' Then he's jest laugh at me as we rolled and looped all over the sky! I shore were skeered! Before anything hurtful happened, he'd take control again and land."

"Wow, John, I'm surprised you ever wanted to have anything to do with airplanes after that."

"Naw, it were excitin'. After a while I got so's I could keep that old plane pretty level. I wanted to larn to land, but Uncle Orv wouldn't never let me try. He said that as a pilot, I was a great mechanic."

"That's cool, but how did uncle Orville learn to fly?" I asked.

"I was about to get to that.", John replied as he tossed the apple core out the window and reached into another pocket for the old corncob pipe that's his favorite. He filled it from the stash of bakker, as he calls it that is tucked in yet another pocket. After much mashing it down, he struck a match on the seat of his coveralls, and with a great show of huffing and puffing, soon got the bakker to smoldering. When he was satisfied that it would keep burning, he continued where he had left off. "Uncle Orv learned from his dad, Wilber,"

"That's really interesting." Then I asked, "But how did Wilber learn?"

"Most folks don't know what I'm about to relate to ya. Back before Mr. Meyer built the airport, there was already a little airstrip. There was a couple of young men that would come here for vacations in the summer. They stayed in an old cabin down near where the airfield is now. Back then there warn't nothin' but a big empty field there. They used to bring a contraption they were working on to the field. It was one of them gliders they was trying to make fly. There warn't no wind in the summers, so they had a hard time figurin' it out. Wilber's dad, Otis, thought he could help. He loaned them his old plow horse to pull the thing up in the air. Bet ya can't guess who those boys were."

"Was it Wilber and Orville Wright?"

"Yep!" my friend exclaimed, "Otis was so impressed that he named his son after Wilber Wright, and Wilber named his son after

Orville Wright."

"So, Otis learned to fly from the Wright Brothers?"

"No young-un! Don't be silly. There warn't no airplane to larn in then. Just that glider. The brothers messed around with it until they finally figured out how to get it up and control it, but Otis jest couldn't keep hangin' around to pull them up for the rest of the summer. That's when they moved on down to Kitty Hawk and became famous."

"But John, that still doesn't explain how your uncle Orville learned to fly."

"Dang it young-un, don't get yer long johns all bunched up!" John exclaimed indigently, "I was jest gettin' to that right now!"

My friend was stomping around and knocking his pipe against his gnarled old hand. "Now look what you've done. Ya made my pipe go out!"

I waited while he dug down into the brown stained pocket of his bib coveralls for another fist full of bakker, stuffed it into the bowl of his pipe, dropping most of it on the ground. Then he dug his grubby hand into the red flannel shirt, first in one pocket, then another and finally produced a kitchen match which he struck against the seat of his pants, and with much grumbling, swearing, huffing, and puffing; he finally he finally succeeded in getting a wisp of smoke curling out of the bowl. When he was satisfied, he carried on. By now his white jacket was covered with brown stains and his tie was all "whopper-jawed", and his hat had fallen off and was on the seat behind him, but he didn't seem to care, or even notice.

"The boys were so grateful for Otis' help that a few years later they came back to Hendersonville wlth a new Wright Flyer and gave it to Otis' young son, Wilber, who was 12 years old at the time, and taught him to fly. And that's how it all came about. Wilber later taught Orville, and Uncle Orville taught me."

"Wow! So, in a way, it was the Wright Brothers who were responsible for your interest in airplanes and for you going into the navy. And now you have this old engine to remind you of it all. You must be very proud." By now we had reached the airfield and I looked over to my old friend, but John was slouched down in the seat with his head against the door post, and the pipe dangling from the corner of his mouth. He was fast asleep.

15. APPLE JOHN'S FAMOUS RELATIVE
(Another Relatively True Apple John Story)

Apple John came to town recently for one of his infrequent visits, and I asked him to read my latest cruising story, *"Old Codger Visits the Coast"*. As he was reading, he commented on the name of the creek that flows along the Beaufort, NC waterfront. It is named Taylor Creek.

"Did ya know that Taylor Creek is named after one of the same pirates that wrecked during a storm way back in colonial times?"

"No, John, I didn't know that. Tell me about it."

At that, my friend pulled out his favorite corncob pipe, knocked out the burned ashes, pulled a new wad of baccer from the pocket of his old, worn-out flannel shirt, and commenced stuffing it in the bowl with the horny little finger of his left hand. Sniffing, snorting, and puffing, he finally got his pipe lit, and amidst a great cloud of smoke, he began his story. "Well, young-un, do y'all remember when I told ya about the feller that discovered the bean plant that Vienna Sausages are made from?"

"Sure, I do," I replied. "I even wrote all about it in my story, *The True History of Vienna Sausage,* but what does that have to do with Taylor Creek?"

John wrinkled up his nose and spat a massive glob of baccer juice on the ground like he always did before relating a great nugget of knowledge. I was glad we were sitting outside! "I never told ya that the feller was a cousin of mine. His name was Thomas Taylor. When most of the crew from the wrecked ship traveled across the Carolina colony to these here mountains, Thomas stayed behind. It was him that had discovered the tasty bean the Indians grew near the hog farm that he was wandering in."

"No, John, I didn't know his name."

I should interrupt the smooth flow of my story right now to suggest to you, my reader, to find my historical account "The True History of Vienna Sausage".

John carried on from there, "As you'll remember, the beans, when soaked in salt water scooped up from the hog farms that were flooded during the frequent storms and hurricanes that ravaged the coast back in them-thar days, became the first commercial crop of the Carolina colony."

"I know all that", I replied, "But it still doesn't explain about Taylor Creek"

"Dang it all, jest be patient and listen! Ya jest might larn a thing or two about a thing or two!"

I'd better explain that old John has gotten pretty cranky in his old age. But he settles down quickly and usually carries on between crotchety outbursts.

"Ya know how pirates would be away from shore for long periods of time. Well, they'd get to missin' girls a whole lot. The first thing they'd do when they got back to dry land was to go a-lookin' for female companionship. Thomas warn't no different. It jest so happens that the first Indian bean farmer he met had a fair young maiden daughter, and as nature goes, Thomas and the girl met, and it whar love at first sight. A son soon came along, and the young couple named him Thomas, Jr. But he was always referred to as Little Tommy. Tommy is the one who finally worked with Gov'nor Eden to build the first Vienna sausage factory."

But John, that's all very interesting, but you still haven't explained why the creek was called Taylor Creek.

With that, John exploded out of his chair, shook his clenched fist in my face, and hollered, "DANG IT ALL, YOUNG-UN, IF YOU'LL JUST SHET UP AND LISTEN, I'LL TELL YA!" After stomping around in circles a few times, he spat out some more baccer juice, and settled back into his chair again. I see that I forgot to tell you that he had dispensed with his pipe, shoving it in a back pocket of his coveralls, and pulled another big wad of tobacco from his pocket, and stuffed it between his cheek and gums.

He eventually picked up where he had left off, "Now I'm about to tell ya about Taylor Creek. The young couple had been given a stretch of land along the creek by his father-in-law as a wedding present. As time went by, Thomas gave young Tommy the land, and it was Tommy who expanded the family bean farming business."

"Awww, c'mon John, how come I've never heard this before?"

"It's been a family secret for all these years, but I guess thar's no reason I cain't tell ya now." As I told ya, Blackbeard had joined up with Governor Eden to can the beans and distribute them throughout the Caribbean. Obviously, the governor couldn't reveal that he was working with the most notorious pirate of the day. And Blackbeard couldn't reveal that he spent time where he could be caught, so they needed someone to actually be the one to do the canning. They soon settled upon Little Tommy."

"Tommy was a very shy boy, but everyone liked him. What people was surprised by, was that Tommy was a genius in business. Not long after he took over the bean farm, his wife's father sold him the rights to all of the hog-waste from the Indians along the creek. It warn't long after this that Blackbeard was captured up at Okrecoke. Tommy had been keepin' a keen eye on the pirate's sausage distribution and knew the pirate captains that were connected with that end of the business. He convinced the governor to allow him to offer safe dockage along his waterfront, along with an official government pardon for the pirates as long as they only carried sausage, and didn't go a-piratin' no more."

"WOW, John", I exclaimed! "I've never heard any of this before."

"And that ain't all", my old friend continued, "Between the bean farm, waste reclamation, and sausage distribution jobs, Tommy was able to hire most everyone that was wantin' to work. At one time, most all of the men and boys from Beaufort and the surrounding areas worked in 'Tommy's Sausage Industries' as he called his new endeavor. And this whar a time when the rest of the colony was in a recession."

So, with a big grin, John wrapped it all up by saying, "Since Tommy owned most all of the land on both sides of the creek, and most of the men from them parts worked for him, the grateful folks jest decided to name the creek for him. 'Little Tommy Taylor Creek' it was called, but before long,

it was jest shortened to 'Taylor Creek'".

"That's quite a story, John, and explains how Taylor Creek got its name, but just one more thing I don't understand. You just said that Tommy owned the land on both sides of the creek. What in the world did he want with the island?"

"Oh, I guess I forgot to tell ya that part.," John said, taking up the story again. "I told ya Tommy was a very smart business man. He was always lookin' for ways to diversify. He started the first terrapin hatchery on the island that had previously been cultivated for growing carrots. He was so captivated by the idea that anyone would be so foolish as to try to grow carrots on the place, that he named it 'Carrot Island'. And now, young-un, you know the entire story about my famous long-ago cousin."

16. APPLE JOHN AND THE BABY CHICKEN
(A Story For The Birds)

It was another warm spring day when I made my way out to World's Edge to visit my old friend Apple John. I found him behind his cabin working on some kind of a fenced area where he was stapling a roll of chicken wire to some new, freshly cut posts that he apparently had dug holes for to make a pen all the way across the back of the cabin. Inside was a little dilapidated shed-like building built on top of sections of partly rotten logs stood on end. I could see that he'd repaired parts of the building where some of the rough-cut boards that it was constructed of, had rotted through. Some had been replaced with fresh wood while others had sections of old corrugated tin roofing nailed over the holes. There was a small opening in one end, with a board with one end on the ground and the other angled up to and resting on the floor in the doorway. There were small strips of wood nailed crossways on the board spaced every foot or so apart. Some of them were old like the shed, while some were new. The roof was made of cedar shakes like John's cabin. As like the rest of the structure, some appeared original while others were new.

"Hey John, what are you building?"

I guess he hadn't heard me approaching as he jumped, turning in the air swinging his arms over his head and slinging the hammer high in the air. He let out a screech and hollered, "Dang-it-all young-un— don't 'cha know better than to sneak up on a body like that!"

I apologized and then just stood quietly as John stamped around as he dug into the pocket of his faded, ragged old flannel shirt for a fist full of baccer that he proceeded to poke into the bowl of his pipe. I recognized the shirt as his favorite red one that he always wore. He's worn it so long that it has faded to a dingy pink.

I chuckled to myself watching him search various other pockets for the kitchen matches he kept in a little pouch that he once told me his pappy had made from the skin of a timber rattler that had dared to bite him. Pappy had dispatched the snake and skinned it on the spot.

John told me that his pappy had been bitten so many times that he was immune to the venom!

"So, what are you working on?"

"What does it look like to you?" John spat out at me. He gets cranky when he's startled.

"Well, I guess it's a chicken coop—isn't it?"

He'd managed to get his pipe lit by now after striking the match on the seat of his coveralls. I noticed it wasn't one of the pipes I'd seen him with over the years I'd known him. It looked like it had been carved out of some kind of stone. "Where'd you get that pipe, John? I don't think I've ever seen it before."

"Well of course you ain't," he replied, "It's an old Indian pipe I found down at the swimmin' hole on the Big Hungry. It's made of soap stone. I found it while I was lookin' for arrow heads."

I knew my old friend collected "points" as they are called by collectors. Most are not arrow heads at all, but spear points, dart points used with an "Atlatl", drills, and scrapers or knives. I'd become interested in collecting native American artifacts myself because of John.

I see I've wandered away from the point of this story---pun intended. So, let's get back to the narrative.

"I didn't know you ever had chickens. Are you planning to get some now?" I asked.

"It's been a powerful long time since I had any." John answered, "But my old Pappy always kept a mess of 'em. When I was a young-un, it was my job to collect the eggs every day. I loved them chick-ons." That's how he pronounced "chicken". "They was my best friends. There warn't no other kids around back then to play with."

"No other kids?" I exclaimed, "I didn't have many friends, but I did always have a best friend."

John looked a little sad as he told me, "I played with the chick-ons all the time. I used to let them out of the coop and we'd chase each other all around the yard. Then they'd get plumb wore out and skedaddle into the crab apple orchard my pappy had and sprawl out under the trees to cool off."

I told my friend that I was glad he had so many chickens for friends. But why was he looking so sad.

"I really miss them chick-ons. One time them chick-ons led me out into the orchard and I fell asleep under the big ol' oak tree that was in the middle. Pappy and mama got to missin' me and came alookin' for me. They found me roostin' among the chick-ons. When Pappy found me, he gave me a mighty big fussin' out, I tell ya!"

"Oh-no! I'm sorry about that. That must have hurt your feelings."

"My favoritest friend came over to find me and made me feel better."

I told John that I thought he didn't have any friends—especially a best friend.

John explained, "My best friend was Woochster. Back then, I liked to scurry up inta the branches of the oak tree to rest. Woochster always flew up and sat next to me. He even sang with me. I taught him how to sing *Just Over in Gloryland.* That was my favorite song I learned in Sunday school in the old *First Big Hungry Snake Handlin Foot Stompin Church* before they done quit using the *Authorized Southern King James Bible* and commenced to singin' that new-fangled devil's music.

"C'mon John, you're just pulling my leg now!"

"Nope, he could kinda crow the notes out. Sounded better than my Auntie Nettie that was leading the choir in them days." He grinned with that.

"That's really cool, John. I bet you had lots of fun with Woochster."

"I shore done that alright. Anytime I was out thar with them chick-ons, he was right thar with me." As John finished telling me that, he had that sad look again and tears were making streaks in the sawdust on his face.

"What's the matter, John, why are you crying?"

"I ain't a-cryin'! I got sawdust in my eye!" He replied crankily.

81

"Awww, dang it all anyway! I came home from church one Sunday and couldn't find Woochster anywhere. I looked all over and still couldn't find him. I even looked out in the oak tree. About then Mama called me in for dinner. Aunt Nettie had come for her birthday. Mama had made Auntie her favorite—chicken dumplins." At this point, John broke down and sobbed, "It was my best friend Wooster—he gave his life to make them dumplins!"

We sat quietly while my friend got himself under control. Finally, he straightened up and chuckled. "I was jest thinkin' about somethin' funny that happened when I was mebbe about nine or ten years old. My Pappy said I was only knee high to a toad stool." That set him off with more laughter interspersed with coughing. When he finally wound down, he began his story.

"Did I ever tell ya the story about how I saved a baby chick-on's life?" He squinted at me as I shook my head no, then picked up again. "Every year Pappy would save out a few eggs to hatch baby chick-ons to replace the ones we'd et for dinner during the last year. My job was to take care of the little chicks."

Right there he stopped again, jumped up, and pointed his bony pointer finger straight at my face. "HEY! that's yore name! Yore a big CHICK-on!" He slapped his knee and began dancing around and clucking loudly! "Cluck-cluck-cluck---BAUCK-BAUCK-BAUCK!!!"

"Cut it out John, that's what the kids do at church when they hear my name for the first time. Just get on with your story."

"Aww, you jest ain't got no sense of funny!"

"This one time I was watchin' the little ones playing in the yard when I noticed this one little bratty chick tryin' to peck the other little chick-ons on their little heads near their eyes. I chased him away, but he kept comin' back and doin' the same dang thing. I told Pappy about it. When he saw the chick peck the others, he said he warn't gonna put up with that and he would wring its scrawny little neck!"

"I remember asking Pappy if I could try to teach it a lesson so it would quit pecking. I put the pecking chick into another coop with some half-grown chick-ons. I thought that the experience would make it homesick to be with its fellow baby chick-ons."

"While I was watching them, that little brat actually jumped and pecked one of the larger chick-ons below its beak. The big chick-on got mad and pecked the little one on top of its hard little head. The baby cheeped for a long time from the pain, but I left it in with the big chick-ons for a while to let it larn its lesson."

"After a while, when I thought it had larnt it's lesson, I took it out and put it back in with its brethren chicks and it apparently had larnt its lesson. It had stopped pecking the others."

"I called Pappy to come watch how the baby chick-on was behaving. Pappy was satisfied that it had learned how to behave itself so he let it live. That little bit of pain and punishment changed its behavior and spared its life."

As he finished, my old friend broke down again. Through his tears, he choked out, "That baby chick grew up to be my best friend Woochster."

17. APPLE JOHN AND A FROSTY MORNING
(A Really Cold Apple John Story)

It was a cold morning in Henderson County and I was staying inside where it was warm. I was snuggled up under a comforter in my recliner watching *Forbidden Planet*, when our little yappy dog, Pepper, flew off my lap and ran to the window yapping her little head off! What now---an Amazon delivery? Another neighborhood dog barking? A squirrel? As I was about to get up, I heard a tapping on the window. I hopped out of my chair, getting tangled in the comforter, and stumbled across the floor to the window. To my surprise, standing outside was my old friend, Apple John.

"John, why are you here? How'd you get here?" I asked. John has only been to my house a couple of times over the years that I've known him. And then only when I brought him. I had no idea he'd even be able to remember how to get here.

"I need yer help, young-un," he exclaimed in his raspy voice. The many years of constant pipe smoking had about ruined his throat.

"Well, come on in, John. Warm yourself while I get my coat."

"We gotta hurry! There ain't much time." He said as he pushed past me and turned repeating, "Gotta go -- GOTTA GO!"

"Ok, I'm coming, but how did you get here?" I asked as we hurried out the door. "And, how DID you get here?"

"On my old scooter. You've never seen it. It's been in the chicken coop since I brought it home with me when I got out of the navy. I ain't never needed it. Horse takes me wherever I need to go, but he's takin' a bit lame. I drug it out and got it runnin' a few days ago. It was all mommicked up."

John was good with what he calls "chinery". He was an aircraft mechanic during the Viet Nam war on the USS Crashalot. The Crashalot was a sort of aircraft carrier. It only had one plane, a Piper J3 Cub. That was the plane he kept flight ready. He also took care of the boat's engine and any other machinery that needed repairs or maintenance.

"We gotta GO!" he repeated yet again. "We need your truck. Help me load this dang scooter in back."

There is no arguing with old John, especially when he is so worked up. I helped him with his scooter, an old Vespa. When I asked my friend about it, he explained that it was a 1947 model. That was the first year they were manufactured. It was kept aboard the Crashalot for trips into town for supplies. It originally had a side car, but John had left it behind when he was discharged. The captain had let John have the Vespa in thanks for his service. The navy had just acquired a second-hand jeep to be used to do what the Vespa had previously been used for.

My old friend was out of breath and I had to help him into the truck. I let him catch his breath before asking what he needed.

After a minute or two, John pointed out the window saying, "Home. We gotta go back to my place. HURRY!"

As we pulled out of my driveway I asked again, "What do you need? Why are you in such a hurry?"

By now, John had caught his breath and was able to continue. "There's gonna be a bad frost tonight. I gotta protect my apple blossoms."

"What apple blossoms? All you have are those straggly old crab apple trees. You never worried about them before."

I knew that he had a small orchard of them behind his cabin. He used to joke that they were cast-offs that old Johnny Appleseed had tossed out because they weren't good enough to spread over the countryside as the legend claims.

"Y'all don't know nothin' 'bout these here apple trees. I've been hiding them. I don't want no kids acomin' on my property and stealin' apples off'n 'em."

John is full of surprises. I had to ask, "But why do you have more apple trees anyway? Where'd you get them?"

My old friend scrunched up his face and replied, "Dang government has cut back on my veteran payments again. I cain't get by no more." (Actually, John sometimes uses saltier language than "dang", but I've cleaned it up for my readers.)

I knew that he's been selling crab apples in town whenever he can to supplement his government income. "So, you got more trees to be able to sell more apples?" I asked.

"Yep, I shore done that." John said. "This is the first year there's gonna be a crop."

"So, what's the problem?"

"That guy on the radio said there'll be a bad frost t'night. I'm a-gonna lose all them apples!" John exclaimed waving his arms around.

"Oh, I see, but what do you need me for? But I'll be glad to help if I can."

"We gotta blow the frost away!"

"What? How can we do that?" I couldn't see what in the world my friend was talking about. Sometimes he gets some crazy ideas.

"Ain't nuttin' to it. Ya know that old Piper engine I brung home from the war?" John said as he started to settle down again.

Maybe some of my faithful readers will remember my story, *"Apple John Learns to Fly"*, and how John told me about that old engine. I had come to his cabin over in the Big Hungry area and found him working on it. "Sure I do, John, but what has that got to do with the frost?"

"I'm agonna stick it up on a pole to blow the frost away," Was his simple answer, "but I need yer help. We gotta bring it over to the orchard and raise it up on that old oak tree. My old hoss cain't lug it with his lame leg."

"Well, OK. How are we going to do that?" I asked.

"Thar ain't nuttin to it." He repeated. "We're jest gonna load it up in this here truck of yourn and carry it out thar."

"Well, I guess we can do that, but how are we going to get it up on the pole?" I asked.

"Jest don't get yerself all rustled up about that. I've got 'er all figgerd out." John said giving me a look like he thought I was as "dumb as a rock". What could I do. I learned a long time ago to not question old John. He had his ways of doing things. Many times, he has proven that he can do anything he sets his mind to--Usually in ways I thought were impossible.

I backed the truck over to the shed door and we loaded the old engine in the bed. Then John pulled out an unusual pipe that looked like it was made out of stone, fished a wad of "baccer", as he calls tobacco, out of a pocket of the worn-out flannel shirt that he wears summer and winter, and stuffed it in the bowl of the pipe with a bony, brown stained finger, struck a match that he had dug out of another pocket, on the seat of his coveralls, and lit the pipe, huffing and puffing frantically. A big cloud of grey smoke poured out as he climbed into the cab next to me.

"Hey John, what is that pipe? I've never seen it before?" I asked. My friend has a large collection of pipes, many of which he had made himself.

"Yep, it's a new one I jest carved outa soapstone jest like the Indians used to do. I found a broken one down in the crick and copied it." he answered as he looked at it, running his hand over the bowl that looked like a facsimile of a turtle.

"But we gotta hurry! Get this dang truck a-movin'." (Once again, I've inserted "dang" in this fascinating narrative in place of John's more colorful language. I'll keep doing it.)

"But John, I don't know where to go."

John gave me another of his looks as he answered gruffly, "To my apple orchard."

"But John, you never told me where it is. Remember, you said it was a secret."

"Oh yeah," my old friend said sheepishly, "Go over yonder." As he pointed to a worn path leading between the trees to the south of his old cabin. John had inherited an untold number of acres from his granpappy, who had in turn inherited it from ancestors that John says go all the way back to pirates that had escaped here to the mountains during the final days of pirating.

I just continued to follow John's finger until we finally arrived at his hidden orchard. He directed me to stop under an ancient red oak tree that he had cut all of the lower limbs off of on one side, leaving the trunk clear. He also had cut the top off leaving a flat spot on top. Before we even came to a stop, he flung open the door and tumbled out.

"Hurry-up an' help me get this dang motor outa the truck."

So, we did. We drug the old motor out and set it on a plastic apple packing crate he had pulled from a large pile off to the side of the orchard.

"Now what are we going to do?" I asked. He gave me another of his looks as he grumbled, "Don't get yer dang undies in a tangle!" I don't know where my friend gets these little sayings. This was a new one. I suppose they come from his navy days.

I sat down on the tailgate and awaited further developments. John made a lengthy production of dumping the ashes out of his pipe, hitting it against the sole of his worn-out aviator boots that he'd brought back from the Crashalot, and refilling it again from the seemingly unending supply of baccer from his shirt pocket. After lighting it as before, taking an extra deep puff, and blowing a cloud of grey smoke out amidst much coughing and hacking, he exclaimed, "Far-out man! That turns me on!"

Maybe I'd better explain that one. John told me once about a sailor on the Crashalot that was known as "The Hippie". He refused to wear his uniform, wearing instead bell-bottom pants and a flowery shirt. After his shift, he'd retire to his cabin that he shared with three other sailors. He'd open his locker and pull out a water pipe that was filled with wine. He'd fill the bowl with "weed" (marijuana), light it, take a big draw, and amidst much coughing say, "Far-out man! That turns me on!" Then he'd stumble around the cabin until he finally collapsed into his berth fast asleep.

Well, back to the story, "John, I just don't see any way we can get that engine way up there in that tree. I think we'd better figure something different out."

We sat there staring at each other and tossing ideas out, but nothing seemed to be a possible solution. "Dang it, young-un. I brought you 'cause I thought you could holp me. I guess it was a waste of time!" Sprinkled with his colorful 'navy words' he said, "I bet that hippie back on the Crash-a-lot woulda thought of somethin'."

That gave me an idea. I had a friend back in my boat racing days down in Florida who always knew how to solve problems with our race boats. Well, actually, they were great ideas when they worked. When they didn't, we either wrecked our boat or the engine blew up. At any rate, it was worth a try. "Don't worry John. I'm going to call my old buddy, Jack "Quicksilver Quilligan", down in Florida. I bet he'll have an idea. Just sit tight while I give him a call."

Old John glared at me, stood up and stomped around a bit, then sat down on an old tree stump and occupied himself with cleaning out the crusty bowl of his "turtle" pipe, all the while muttering to himself.

Jack answered on the third ring. "Hey Quicksilver, I've got a problem you can help me with." I told him what we were trying to do. I was surprised when he replied without even taking a minute to think.

Chick, you won't believe this, but I read about something in the paper that was almost like your situation. There was a guy named Lawrence in central Florida that wanted to save his oranges from an ensuing freeze. He decided to use his airboat. He thought that with the boat's old Cadillac V8 and a prop, it's a no brainer!"

"What in the world! How did he do that? What does a freezing orange grove have to do with an air boat? That just sounds crazy!"

Jack replied, "You and I know from personal experience that this is just the male gene of 'Inherited stupidity' speaking. Lawrence, you're basic good old "Florida Boy" from central Florida, subjected to way too much sun, beer, and owning an airboat, might not have fully thought this plan through. Not being judgmental; just sayin'."

Jack has a colorful way of telling about things. He continued, "Apparently, when the night of the big freeze came, he attached the airboat with trailer to his Toyota pickup and started the Cadillac V8. His wife was in the pilot seat manning the V8's throttle, etc. At first, all went well. Lawerence left the truck in neutral and the airboat's big Caddy V8 thrust everything forward, including the truck, between the rows of trees. Lawerence said that 'Driving it was just the opposite of backing up a boat trailer. Not too difficult. I just pushed the clutch in, nursed my Bud and steered.'"

"His wife, now being literally the backseat driver, and having never been allowed to pilot the boat in the water, grabbed the rudder and figured, 'Why not give each plant a full shot of warm air?' And this is where Lawerence's plan went south. The boat and trailer started whipping around every which-away, throwing branches and oranges in all directions! Lawrence's brakes didn't do much and Wifie didn't know how to stop the Caddy. The few neighbors watching said the boat, trailer, and pickup combo moved like a snake!"

I had turned the phone's speaker on as Jack related the story and old John had cupped his hand over his ear and listened intently to the whole thing. "Sounds like a whoppin' good plan to me! I know how we can use that idea! We be tons smarter than that old Florida cracker-boy!"

By now John was hopping from one foot to the other and waving his arms around. Ashes from his pipe were flying all around and settling over us both like black snowflakes. I thanked Jack and quickly terminated my call, promising to call back and let Jack know if things went better for us than for poor Lawrence.

"We gotta hurry! We gotta get ready! It's getting' late!"

"I know what you're planning, John, but I'm not going to let you use my truck for this!"

"You don't know nothin'!" John cried, "That dang cracker was dumb as a rock usin' a truck for that! I know a much better way!"

"Ok, what are we going to do?"

"Hurry! Take me back to my cabin! We gotta get my wagon and old Mule!" As I've told you before, my old friend always just names his animals with whatever kind of animal it is. The only exceptions were his coop full of chickens. They all have quaint, old-fashioned southern girl names.

I had no idea what my friend was planning, but I knew better than to waste time trying to ask him. I just got in my truck, and John crawled in the other side. We made our way back to John's cabin with my friend bouncing in his seat and gesticulating with his pipe as he plotted-out the details of his big plan. We hadn't come to a complete stop when he flung the door open, jumped out, and landed flat on his face!

"Settle down, John," I said as I helped him up. "You could have hurt yourself. And look what you did to your pipe." It had broken into several pieces.

"Well, dangedy-dang-dang!" He exclaimed as he brushed himself off. (I've shortened and cleaned up his actual words.) "I'll jest make me a new one! C'mon, help me hitch Mule to the wagon."

We did just that. Then we loaded the Piper motor onto the wagon with the propeller facing the back. "Don't you think we should tie it down? It might fall off.", I said.

"Whaddaya think I'ma getting' ready to do right now!", he said as he rushed into his dilapidated old shed where he stashes just about anything he could ever need. Or think he'd need. It's all crammed together in piles, stacked in corners, and shoved up in the rafters. Soon, there emanated a great crescendo of crashes, banging, and a plethora of "navy words". Then, "I'VE GOT SOMTHIN'!" as he ran out with a roll of barbed wire.

"What's that for, John?" I asked innocently.

"Why, to tie the dang motor on of course!" C'mon and holp me, young-un!

"That's all you could find?", I asked questioningly.

"Shet-up and help!", is all he said as he started twisting the wire around the motor and the boards of the wagon bed. I did what I could, but I wasn't much help with my soft, tender hands. Old John, on the other hand, (pun intended) just grabbed the wire and yanked it in place. The years of hard work had toughened up has hands like old shoe leather. Pretty soon we had the engine strapped down securely and were headed back to his orchard. It was almost dark, and getting cold when we arrived.

"What now, John. That thing is strapped down with so much barbed wire that it's going to be really hard to get it loose. Besides, what are we going to do with it anyway?"

"Are ya crazy!" John bellowed. "Why do ya think I went to so much work to get 'er tied on!"

With that, my friend climbed up on the seat of the wagon and drove the wagon between the first rows of trees. He set the brake of the wagon, which was just a pad of wood that was forced against one of the wheels with a lever.

He hollered, "Hold 'er, Mule!" Then he went back to the engine, opened a valve on the attached fuel tank, turned a switch, walked behind the engine and flipped the prop. The Piper motor started with a roar! Dog let out a pathetic howl as he exploded out from under an apple tree where he'd crawled into the shade for a nap when we had first come here in my truck. I hadn't even missed him.

"You can mosey on home, now," he hollered over the roar of the engine, "I've got this thang." With that, he pulled himself back onto the wagon seat, gave a tug on the reins, and released the brake lever. The wagon gave a jerk and started rushing forward, but John hollered, "Hold 'er back, Mule, and brought the rig under control. I watched for a few minutes, and all was going well, so I got back into my old Dodge truck and "moseyed" on home, just as John told me to.

I know that now is when you expect me to tell you of the disastrous outcome of the story, but I have to report that Apple John and Mule drove that old Piper Cub engine up and down the rows of apple trees all night without incident. The crop was saved. I never should have doubted my old friend.